KU-319-279

JUST MARRIED!

KISS THE BRIDESMAID

BY
CARA COLTER

AND

BEST MAN SAYS I DO

BY
SHIRLEY JUMP

MILLS & BOON

HOUNSLOW LIBRARIES

BEA

C0000 002 474 861

HJ	25-Dec-2009
AF ROM	£3.19
HOUCO	

DID YOU PURCHASE THIS BOOK WITHOUT A COVER?

If you did, you should be aware it is *stolen property* as it was reported *unsold and destroyed* by a retailer. Neither the author nor the publisher has received any payment for this *stripped book*.

All the characters in this book have no existence outside the imagination of the author, and have no relation whatsoever to anyone bearing the same name or names. They are not even distantly inspired by any individual known or unknown to the author, and all the incidents are pure invention.

All Rights Reserved including the right of reproduction in whole or in part in any form. This edition is published by arrangement with Harlequin Enterprises II BV/S.à.r.l. The text of this publication or any part thereof may not be reproduced or transmitted in any form or by any means, electronic or mechanical, including photocopying, recording, storage in an information retrieval system, or otherwise, without the written permission of the publisher.

This book is sold subject to the condition that it shall not, by way of trade or otherwise, be lent, resold, hired out or otherwise circulated without the prior consent of the publisher in any form of binding or cover other than that in which it is published and without a similar condition including this condition being imposed on the subsequent purchaser.

® and TM are trademarks owned and used by the trademark owner and/or its licensee. Trademarks marked with ® are registered with the United Kingdom Patent Office and/or the Office for Harmonisation in the Internal Market and in other countries.

First published in Great Britain 2009
Paperback edition 2010
Harlequin Mills & Boon Limited,
Eton House, 18-24 Paradise Road, Richmond, Surrey TW9 1SR

© Harlequin Books S.A. 2009

The publisher acknowledges the copyright holder of the individual works as follows:

KISS THE BRIDESMAID © Cara Colter 2009
BEST MAN SAYS I DO © Shirley Jump 2009

ISBN: 978 0 263 86968 2

Harlequin Mills & Boon policy is to use papers that are natural, renewable and recyclable products and made from wood grown in sustainable forests. The logging and manufacturing process conform to the legal environmental regulations of the country of origin.

Printed and bound in Spain
by Litografia Rosés, S.A., Barcelona

Dear Reader

I love summer. I love the lemonade, the barbecues, the July fireworks. I love swimming in ice-cold water on simmering hot days, and I love sitting in a comfy chair in the shade with a good book.

No matter what time of year you are reading this story, I hope it gives you that summertime feeling. A feeling of life being fun, and simple, and filled with delightful surprises.

To me, that is the magic of a romance novel. It can transport you, immerse you in a different world, take you from a cold place to the place of endless summer that each of us holds in our hearts. Journey with me now, from wherever you are, to the season of summer and the season of love.

With warmest wishes

Cara Colter

With thanks to Shirley Jump for all her great ideas,
and for sharing her Cape Cod summers.

CHAPTER ONE

"LADIES, if you would gather by the chocolate fountain, Mrs. Charles Weston is about to throw her bouquet." Colton St. John had been best man at the wedding of two of his oldest friends, and now he was acting as the master of ceremonies.

The town had been founded by his forefathers, and leadership came easily to him. At twenty-eight, the dark-haired, blue-eyed Colton would have been a more likely movie star than a law school graduate and the youngest mayor St. John's Cove had ever elected.

Not that Samantha Hall, bridesmaid, was admiring the confidence and finesse of her dear friend, Colton, at the moment.

It's nearly over, she told herself as she slid toward the exit of the St. John's Cove Yacht Club. It was hard to be unobtrusive in the bridesmaid's gown that Amanda—make that *Mrs.* Charles Weston—had chosen. Amanda had glowingly described the color as fuchsia, but it wasn't. The dress was the exact shade of pink Sam's current stray rescued dog, Waldo, had thrown up after eating the Jell-O salad Sam had made for Amanda's bridal shower earlier in the week.

As if the color wasn't hideous enough, Sam considered the dress just a little too *everything* for a wedding. Between hitching up the hem so she wouldn't trip over it, pulling the tiny spaghetti straps back on her shoulders every time they slipped down, and tugging at the plunging V-line of the bodice, the dress had felt like a full-time job since she had first put it on nearly twelve hours ago.

Even her three older brothers, who usually teased unmercifully when she put on "girl" clothes, had gone silent when she had come out to the car and they'd seen the dress for the first time.

"I thought you said it looked like dog puke," her oldest brother, Mitch, had said, holding open the door of his ancient station wagon for her. She was driving with her brothers to the wedding because she couldn't manage the clutch of her Land Rover in the three-inch heels, plus was afraid of splitting the hind end out of the dress getting in and out of her higher vehicle.

And then Mitch had done the oddest thing. He'd kissed her cheek and said, almost sadly, "When did you go and grow up, Sam?"

Since she'd been living in her own apartment above the business she had founded here in St.

John's Cove after graduating from high school seven years ago, his comment had been insulting rather than endearing.

Trust a man! Show a little too much cleavage, pile your hair on top of your head and put on a bit of makeup, and you were all grown-up.

Her brothers' reaction had foreshadowed an uncomfortable evening. Guys she had spent her whole life in this small Cape Cod hamlet with—boating and swimming and fishing—had been sending her sidelong looks as if she'd gone and grown a second head.

Thankfully most of them were too scared of her brothers to do anything about it except gawk.

Though there was one man—he'd been introduced in the reception line on the steps of St. Michael's Church as Amanda's cousin, Ethan Ballard—who hadn't been able to take his eyes off of her through the whole evening.

He was gorgeous, too. Tall, lean, broad-shouldered. Dark. Dark eyes, dark hair.

Sam killed the intrigue he made her feel.

He'd asked her to dance four times, but she'd said no. Even his voice gave her the shivers, deep and measured.

The truth was she didn't know how to dance, and wasn't going to make a fool of herself by trying for the first time in the heels. The truth was, Ethan was asking the illusion to dance. If he'd seen her in her normal duds—rolled-up jeans, sneakers, a faded shirt that advertised her pet store and supply business, Groom to Grow, he would have never looked that interested.

Of course, there was always the possibility one of the local guys had dared him to show interest in her, or offered him twenty bucks to dance with her.

Knowing that any man in St. John's Cove who went near Samantha Hall was going to have to run the gauntlet of her brothers.

Sam glanced over to where Ethan was standing, one shoulder braced against the wall, his tie undone, his crisp white shirt open against the end-of-June early-summer heat in the reception room. He was nursing a drink and *still* looking at her.

And he didn't look like a fool, either. Ethan Ballard radiated the confidence, wealth and poise one would expect from a businessman from Boston.

He raised his glass to her, took a long, slow sip without taking his eyes from her. Now how could that possibly seem suggestive, make her insides melt into hot liquid?

How about because she hadn't had a date in over a year? And that date had been with a *sumpie*—she and her friends' pet name for summer people— because the locals were afraid to ask her out. And with good reason. After one drink, her brother Mitch had shown up at the Clam Digger, glowering and flexing muscles earned from plying his strength and guts against the waters of the Atlantic to make his living as a lobsterman.

To the local male population, she was Sam, not Samantha. She could outrun, outsail and outswim most of them—it was a well-known fact no one had beaten her in a race to the buoys since she was sixteen. But even if the local young men weren't totally intimidated by that, nobody wanted to deal with the Hall brothers, Mitch, Jake and Bryce, when it came to their little sister.

Which was okay with her. Fairy tales had finished for her family when her mom and dad had been killed in a boating accident when she was twelve. Mitch, newly married, had stepped up to the plate and taken in his siblings, but his wife, Karina, had not bargained for a ready-made family of two rowdy teenage brothers, and a twelve-year-old girl swimming in pain. Karina, Sam's one chance for a bit of feminine influence, had jumped ship.

Her brothers had raised her so she could fight but not put on makeup, handle a fishing rod but not wear heels, arm wrestle but not dance. They'd given her an earful about what men *really* wanted.

Plus, all three of her brothers had taken Karina's abandonment personally and were commitment phobic, and so was she.

Most of the time. Occasionally Sam felt this odd little tug of wistfulness. She felt it when she watched couples walk hand in hand along the beach at sunset, she felt it when old Mr. and Mrs. Nelson came into her shop, their teasing affection for one another reminding Sam of her mom and dad.

And Sam had felt it with surprising strength when Charlie and Amanda had exchanged their vows earlier at St. Michael's, Amanda glowing, and Charlie choking up on emotion.

Sam's own eyes had teared up, and she was so unaccustomed to that, she didn't have a tissue, and so unaccustomed to mascara that she didn't know crying in it would have unfortunate consequences.

And she had reacted like that even though she personally felt that if there were ever two people who should not have gotten married, it was Charlie and Amanda!

The pair were part of a tight-knit group of six friends, Colton St. John, Vivian Reilly and Sam's brother Bryce, who had been hanging out together since grade school. Sam was the youngest of the group—she had started as a tagalong with Bryce. Amanda and Charlie had been dating on and off since they were fourteen, their relationship punctuated with frequent drama, constant squabbling, and hundreds of breakups and makeups.

Ah. Sam's hand connected with the steel bar of the exit door of the reception hall. She pushed, caught a whiff of the fresh June breeze coming in off the bay. *Freedom.* On an impulse, she turned and wagged her fingers at Ethan Ballard, *goodbye.*

"Oh, no, you don't," Vivian Reilly said. Vivian, also a charter member of the Group of Six, was the other bridesmaid, and she caught Sam's arm just as she was halfway out the door.

"How come the dress doesn't look like dog puke on you?" Sam asked, wishing she could take back that impulsive wag of the fingers.

The color of the dress should have clashed with Vivian's incredible red hair, but, of course, it didn't. Vivian looked leggy and beautiful, but then Vivian could wear a grain sack and make it look sexy. If anything, the dress was slightly more demure than Vivian's usual style.

"It mustn't look all that bad on you, either," Vivian said with a laugh. "Check out that man staring at you. I'm getting heat stroke from it. He's glorious. Ethan something? Amanda's cousin?"

Ethan Ballard. Sam remembered his name perfectly, not to mention the touch of his hand in that reception line. Lingering. Sam slid Amanda's cousin another look, and looked away, though not before her heart tumbled in her chest, and she felt the tug of something a lot stronger than the wistfulness she felt when she looked at old Mr. And Mrs. Nelson picking out a new collar for their badly spoiled Pom, Duffy.

Ethan Ballard *was* glorious. And no doubt just as superficial as every other guy in the world, including her brothers. She did not kid herself that the good-looking cousin would have given her a second look if her hair was pulled back into its usual no-nonsense ponytail, her eyes were not smudged with the plum shadow that Vivian and Amanda insisted made them look greener, and her chest wasn't falling out of the embarrassingly low-cut dress.

The door clicked shut again, and Sam, resigned, tugged at the dress. She glanced up to see Ethan Ballard watching, an amused smile playing at the handsome, firm line of his wide mouth.

There was that hot rush again, so she stuck her nose in the air so he wouldn't ever guess.

"Come on," Vivian said, steering Sam back toward the gaggle of giggling single girls and women waiting for the traditional throwing of the bouquet. "Be a sport."

Amanda was standing at the front of the room now, still glowing, a queen looking benevolently at her subjects. No doubt she was kidding herself that this was the best day of her life, Sam thought cynically.

As soon as Vivian let go of her arm, Sam moved way up to the front of the gathering of hopefuls. She'd played ball with the bride, and Amanda had a strong throwing arm. As long as she didn't do the I'm-cute-and-helpless routine, that bouquet should sail right over Sam's head and hit old Mable Saunders in the back row.

Sixty and never married.

Which will probably be me someday, Sam thought, and given that she was cynical about the institution of marriage she was not sure why the thought made her feel more wistful—and gloomy—than before.

The truth was the whole day had made her feel gloomy, not just because she didn't hold out much hope for Amanda and Charlie—why would they be the one out of two couples who succeeded when they hadn't ever managed to go more than three days in their whole relationship without a squabble—but because Sam didn't like change.

Her five friends were the unchangeable anchor in her life. Vivian, Amanda, Charles, Colton and Sam's brother Bryce had all hung out together for as long as she could remember. Oh, some of them moved, went to college, came back, but the ties remained unbreakable. The constancy of family and friendships were what made life in the small Cape Cod community idyllic for its three thousand permanent residents.

This was the biggest change they had experienced. A wedding. Sam didn't like it. She didn't like it one bit.

Though she had to admit Amanda did look beautiful in her wedding dress, beaming at them all from the front of the room.

The dress, considering the sudden haste to get married, was like something out of a fairy tale, a princess design of a tight-fitting beaded bodice and full floor-length skirt with about sixty-two crinolines underneath it.

Amanda's eyes met hers, full of mischief, so Sam was relieved when someone suggested Amanda turn around with her back to them all, so she couldn't choose who to toss the bouquet to. As soon as Amanda did turn around, Sam shuffled positions, moving closer to the burbling chocolate fountain, still close to the front, gambling on Amanda's good arm.

What she couldn't have gambled on was this: Amanda threw the bouquet over her shoulder with all her might. It arched up and up and up toward the ceiling.

Those who really were eager to catch the thing moved back in anticipation of where it would fall back to earth.

But the bouquet hit an exposed beam, and instead of completing its arc, it fell straight down like a duck shot out of the sky.

It was going to land right in the middle of the chocolate fountain.

Unless someone intervened.

For an uncharitable moment, Sam swore it was not going to be her.

But she caught a glimpse of the horrified look on Amanda's face and wondered in that split second if it wasn't some kind of bad luck for the bouquet not to be caught, to land smack dab in the middle of a pool of burbling chocolate.

Amanda and Charlie were going to need all the luck they could get.

Reluctantly Sam reached out an arm, and the bouquet fell into her hand as if it had been destined to find her.

A cheer went up, though she could hear the lusty challenge of Mitch.

"Anyone who thinks they're going to marry my sister is going to have to arm wrestle me first."

Sam smiled, with so many teeth she felt like a dog snarling, waved the bouquet and headed for the exit.

So that's my future wife, Ethan Ballard thought, watching the bridesmaid head out the exit onto the stone veranda that faced the sea. He bet she was going to hurl that bouquet right off of there, too. He hadn't missed her thwarted attempt at escape earlier, or the way she had looked during the dinner and the toasts. Cynical. Uncomfortable. Bored.

The least romantic woman in the room. Perfect.

He'd been pretty sure she was the one from the moment he'd laid eyes on her. Despite the sexy outfit, and the abundance of rich chocolate upswept hair, he could tell by the sunburn and freckles that she was the wholesome, outdoorsy type that he imagined the Finkles would love.

She'd be perfect for the task he had in mind. When he'd held her hand a little too long in the reception line she'd yanked it away and given him a dirty look with those sea-mist eyes of hers.

Ditto for his offers to dance with her. Though

Ethan felt faintly stung—who didn't want to dance with *him*—it boded well for his plan.

Samantha Hall was the girl least likely to appreciate his offer of marriage. Least likely to want anything else once the assignment was over.

And he only needed a wife for one day.

Tomorrow. Combining his cousin Amanda's wedding with business, Ethan was in Cape Cod looking at real estate. He'd seen a promising property on the Main Street of St. John's Cove this morning, but what he really wanted was an old family cottage up the coast, between St. John's and Stone Harbor. He'd been drooling over the Internet pictures of Annie's Retreat for over a week, and had an appointment to see it tomorrow.

Then his lawyer had called. He'd done his homework, as always. The current owners, the Finkles, had turned down a lot of offers on the place. They knew exactly what they wanted, and it wasn't to sell to a businessman who would see their property as an investment, who would see the development potential in that rare amount of oceanfront.

The Finkles would be more amenable to an offer made by Mr. and Mrs. Ballard, who wanted to raise a dozen children on the place.

Trying not to whistle at his good fortune in finding the perfect Mrs. Ballard so quickly, Ethan headed out the door after her. Job one was to find out if she knew the Finkles. If she did, he wouldn't proceed.

Samantha Hall was in the shadows, on the wide deck behind the exit door, standing so still that for a moment he didn't see her. And when he did he was struck by her loveliness, her slender figure silhouetted by moonlight, her face lifted to the breeze.

She was looking out at the sailboats and yachts bobbing in their moorings, something faintly wistful in her expression.

Very romantic.

She turned, startled when she heard him come out, turned away instantly. He almost laughed out loud when she pulled at the front of her dress, *again*. The dress fit her graceful lines perfectly and showed off her slender curves to mouthwatering advantage.

But for some reason he found her discomfort with it far more delightful than the dress itself.

"Gorgeous night," he said conversationally.

"Hmm." Noncommittal. *Suspicious*.

"Lucky catch on the bouquet."

"I guess that depends what you think lucky is."

"Isn't the one who catches it the next one to get married?" he asked.

"There's a disclaimer clause if you're just saving the bouquet from a disastrous dip in chocolate."

Ethan laughed, and not just because it was the perfect answer for a man with a mission like his.

"What did you do with the bouquet?" he asked.

Her eyes slid guiltily to the left and he saw the

bridal bouquet had been shoved in a planter, the elegant lilies bright white against red geraniums.

"I'm Ethan Ballard," he said, extending his hand.

"We met in the reception line," she said, pretending she didn't see it.

The music started inside. He wondered if he should ask her to dance, *again,* and was surprised that he wanted to dance with her. But on the other hand, there was no sense romancing her. His marriage proposal wasn't about romance, and he didn't want her to think it was.

Job one, he reminded himself, surprised at how hard it was to get down to business with her scent tickling at his nostrils.

"Do you know a family named the Finkles, over Stone Harbor way?" he asked.

Her brow scrunched in momentary concentration. "No," she said. "I can't say I do." Then, with a touch of defensiveness, "My world is pretty small. You're looking at it." And she nodded her chin toward the sea and then the barely visible lights of town.

"I'm looking for a wife," he said, always the businessman, cutting to the chase, even while he kept his tone light, and even while he was aware of being not completely professional. A renegade part of him was looking forward to getting to know her a tiny bit better.

She shot him a look. "Goodie for you."

Despite the fact this was all a business venture for

him, he was a little taken aback at her lack of interest in him. That was not the reaction he got from women at all. Obviously she had no idea who he was, and he found that in itself refreshing.

What would it be like to get to know another human being who didn't know you were heir to a fortune, a millionaire businessman in your own right and a retired major league baseball player?

"You caught the bouquet, it seemed fortuitous. I have a proposition for you," he said carefully.

"Propose away," she said, but he realized when she tucked a wayward strand of her glossy dark hair behind her ear that she was not as cavalier about his attention as she wanted him to believe.

For the first time, he felt a moment's hesitation. Maybe she wasn't right for this job, after all; there was something sweetly vulnerable under all that not very veiled cynicism.

At that moment the side door exploded open. His cousin, Amanda, came bursting out, the skirt of her bridal confection caught in her hands, tears streaming down her face. She raced down the stairs with amazing swiftness given that her outfit was not exactly designed for a one-hundred-yard dash. She was at the bottom of the stairs before the door exploded open again, and Charlie came out it.

"Mandy, honey, come on. Don't be like this."

"Don't you Mandy, honey, me!" she yelled, rounding on him. "How could you?"

Ethan was pretty sure that neither of them had even noticed that he and Samantha were in the shadows behind the door. Samantha had gone still as a statue, and he did the same.

And then the bride turned around, tore past the pier, up a set of stairs on the other side of it and into the parking lot. Charlie gained on her and caught her; a furious discussion ensued that Ethan felt grateful he could not hear.

The discussion resulted in Amanda climbing behind the wheel of her bright yellow sports car convertible, revving the engine and leaving Charlie in a splatter of gravel.

Ethan turned to see how his bridesmaid reacted to the drama. She was leaning on the railing, her small chin on her hands, a knowing little smile playing sadly on her lips as she gave her head a cynical shake.

His doubt of a moment earlier was erased. *She was perfect.*

"Will you marry me?" he asked.

"Why not?" she answered, then smirked at his startled expression. "We have at least as good a chance as them."

And then she looped her arm through his and dragged him back through the door, he suspected so that Charlie, who was coming back up the steps, shoulders drooping, would remain unaware that the horrible little wedding-night drama had had witnesses.

Ethan was struck by how the sensitivity of the gesture, the loyalty to her friends, did not match the cynicism she was trying to display.

She could have saved herself the effort, though. Back inside it was evident the bride and groom had had many witnesses to their first argument as a married couple.

"About my proposal," Ethan told her, taking her elbow and looking down at her, "I'll make it worth your while."

She smiled sweetly at him. "Believe me, it already is."

And that's when he saw a mountain of a man moving toward him, a scowl on his face that could mean nothing but trouble.

CHAPTER TWO

"YOUR boyfriend?" Ethan asked Samantha.

"Worse," she told him, still smiling sweetly at him. "My brother." She reached up and brushed her lips on his, he presumed to make sure he was really in trouble.

But the kiss took them both by surprise. He could tell by the way her eyes widened, and he felt a thrilled shock at the delicacy of those lips touching his, too.

But she backed away rapidly, wiped her mouth with the back of her hand. "And that will teach you to take twenty bucks to pretend you're interested in me. Oh, hi, Mitch, this is Ethan. He just asked me to marry him."

Then she wagged her fingers at him and disappeared into the throng of people milling about discussing the tiff between the bride and groom.

Her lips, Ethan thought, faintly dazed, had tasted of strawberries and sea air.

He watched her go, troubled not so much by the impending arrival of her brother, as by the fact she thought someone would have to pay him to show interest in her, and that she thought, even on the shortness of their acquaintance, that he would be such a person.

Of course, he was trying to buy a bride, not exactly a character reference.

The man stopped in front of him and folded ham-sized hands over a chest so wide it was stretching the buttons on his dress shirt.

"I've got a question for you," Mitch said menacingly.

In a split second an amazing number of possibilities raced through Ethan's mind. *What were you doing outside with my sister? What are your intentions? Why are you kissing someone you just met? You asked my sister to marry you?* None of the answers Ethan came up with boded well for him.

He braced himself. Ethan did not consider himself a fighter, but he wasn't one to back down, either.

"You really are Ethan Ballard, aren't you?"

The question was so different than what he was bracing himself for that Ethan just nodded warily.

"I gotta know why you left the Sox. One season. No injury. Great rookie year. I gotta know."

Despite the menace, Ethan felt himself relax. He could tell Samantha's brother was one of those hard-working, honest men that these communities, once all fishing villages, were famous for producing.

Ethan had his stock answer to the question he had

just been asked, but he surprised himself by not giving it. In a low voice he said, "I wanted to be liked and respected for who I was, not for what I did."

A memory, painful, squeezed behind his eyes, of Bethany saying, her voice shrill with disbelief, *You did what?* And that had been the end of their engagement, just as his father had predicted.

Samantha's brother regarded him thoughtfully for a moment, made up his mind, clapped him, hard, on the shoulder. "Come on. I'll get you a beer and you can meet my brothers."

"About that marriage proposal—"

The big man's eyes sought his sister and found her. He watched her for a moment and then sighed.

"Don't worry. I know she was just kiddin' around, probably kissed you to get me mad, as if I could get mad at Ethan Ballard. Nobody's gonna marry my little sister."

"Why's that?" Ethan asked, and he felt troubled again. Samantha Hall was beautiful. And had plenty of personality and spunk. Why would it seem so impossible that someone—obviously not a complete stranger who had just met her, but someone—would want to marry her?

"They'd have to come through me first," Mitch said, and then, "And even if they didn't, she'd have to find someone who is more a man than she is. My fault. I raised her. Don't be fooled by present appearances. That girl is as tough as nails."

But it seemed to Ethan what Samantha Hall needed was not someone who was more a man than her at all. It was someone who saw the woman in her. And who could clearly see she was not tough as nails. He thought of the softness of her lips on his and the vulnerability he had glimpsed in her eyes when he had joined her outside. And he wondered just what he was getting himself into, and why he felt so committed to it.

Sam couldn't believe it. A complete stranger had asked her to marry him. She knew Ethan Ballard was kidding—or up to something—but her heart had still gone crazy when he had said the words! Having been raised by brothers, Sam knew better than to let her surprise or intrigue show. There was nothing a man liked better than catching a woman off guard to get the upper hand!

She was annoyed to see her brothers *liked* him. She watched from across the room as they gathered around him, as if he was a long-lost Hall, clapping him on the shoulder and offering him a beer. Ethan Ballard had wormed his way into their fold effortlessly.

Well, she thought, *that's a perfect end to a perfect day.* Her feet hurt, she was tired of the dress and she felt sick for Charlie and Amanda. Fighting on a wedding night had to be at least as bad for luck as the bouquet not getting caught. Sam had just postponed the inevitable by making her heroic save.

Still, her work here was done. Much as she would have liked to know what that proposal was really about, she didn't want Ethan Ballard to think she cared! No, better to leave him thinking she shrugged off marriage proposals from strangers as if they were a daily occurrence!

Sam made her way to the front door and finally managed to get away. Outside, she kicked off her heels and went around the parking lot toward the yacht club private beach that bordered it, the shortest route back to the small hamlet of St. John's Cove.

"Hey!"

Samantha turned and saw Ethan Ballard coming toward her, even his immense confidence no match for the sand. If she ran, he'd never catch her. But then he might guess he made her feel afraid in some way she didn't quite understand.

Not afraid of him. But afraid of herself.

She thought of the way his lips had felt when she had playfully brushed them with hers, and she turned and kept walking.

He caught up to her anyway.

"I see you survived my brothers."

"You sound disappointed."

"They usually run a better defense," she said. She could feel her heart pounding in her chest, and she was pretty sure it wasn't from the exertion of walking through the sand.

"Where are you going?" he asked.

A different girl might have said, *Midnight swim, skinny-dipping,* but she couldn't. She didn't quite know what to make of his attention. She was enjoying it, and *hating* the fact she was enjoying it. "Home."

"I'll walk you."

No one *ever* walked her anywhere. She was not seen as the fragile type; in fact her bravery was legend. She was the first one to swim in the ocean every year, she had been the first one out of the plane when the guys had talked her into skydiving. When they were fourteen and had played chicken with lit cigarettes, she had always won. She was known to be a daredevil in her little sailboat, an old Cape Dory Typhoon named the *Hall Way.*

Sam was a little taken aback that she *liked* his chivalry. So she said, with a touch of churlishness, "I can look after myself."

"I'll walk you home, anyway."

There was nothing argumentative in his tone. Or bossy. He was just stating a fact. He was walking her home, whether she liked it or not.

And she certainly didn't want him to know that she did like that feeling of being treated as fragile and feminine.

"Suit yourself."

He stopped after a moment, slid off his shoes and socks. Since she was stuck with him anyway, she waited, admiring the way he looked in the moon-light, silver beams tangling in the darkness of his hair, his now bare feet curling into the sensuousness of the sand.

He straightened, shoes in hand, and she saw the moonlight made his dark eyes glint with silver shadows, too.

She started walking again, and he walked beside her.

"Do you want to talk about the proposal?"

A renegade thought blasted through her of what it would be like to actually be married to a man like him. To taste those lips whenever you wanted, to feel his easy strength as part of your life.

Maybe that's why Amanda and Charlie had rushed to get married even when the odds were against them, pulled toward that soft feeling of not being alone anymore.

"I already said I'd marry you," she said, her careless tone hiding both her curiosity and the vulnerability those thoughts made her feel. "My brothers, strangely enough, liked you. What's to discuss?"

He laughed, and she didn't feel like he was laughing at her, but truly enjoying her. It would be easy to come to love that sensation. Of being *seen*. And appreciated.

"Setting a date?" he kidded.

"Oh. I guess there's that. How about tomorrow?" She reminded herself most of his appreciation was thanks to the costume: the dress and the hair and the makeup.

"I'm free, and by happy coincidence that's when I need a wife. Just for the day. Want to play with me?"

The awful thing was she *did* want to play with him, desperately. But what she considered playing—a day of sailing or swimming—was probably not what he considered playing. At all. His next words confirmed that.

"I'm a real estate investor. I buy higher end properties that have gone to seed, fix them up and flip them."

Oh, he *played* with money.

"I thought the market was gone," she said. She thought of the real estate sign hanging in front of her own rented premises, and thanked the wedding for its one small blessing.

She hadn't thought of *that* all day.

Because ever since the sign had gone up, she'd been getting stomachaches. Her business relied on its prime Main Street, St. John's, location, the summer people coming in and buying grooming supplies, the cute little doggy outfits she stocked, the good-grade dog foods, the amazing and unusual pet accessories that she spent her spare time seeking out. But she knew she'd been getting an incredible deal on the rent, which included her storefront and the apartment above it. A new owner meant one of two things, neither of them good. She would be paying higher rent, or she would get evicted.

"I'm in a position where I can buy and hold if I have to," he said with easy self-assurance, "though the market is never really gone for the kind of clients who buy my properties."

"Oh," she said. He dealt with the old rich, like the St. John family who had founded this town.

"One of my scouts called in a property down the coastline from here a few miles, a little closer to Stone Harbor than here. It's ideal—beachfront, a couple of acres, an old house that needs to be torn down or extensively remodeled, I'm not sure which yet."

The private beach they were walking down intersected with a boardwalk. Sam leaned over to put on her shoes to protect her feet from splinters on the weathered old boardwalk. When she raised up one foot, she took an awkward step sideways in the sand.

She felt a thrilled shock when Ethan reached out quickly to steady her, his one hand red-hot on her naked shoulder, his other caressing as he took her remaining shoe from where she was dangling it from its strap in her hand. He slid it onto her foot, his palm cupping the arch for a suspended second before sliding away.

He stepped away from her, acted as if nothing had happened as he sat down and put on his own socks and shoes.

How could he possibly not have felt that current that leaped in the air between them when he touched her foot? His touch had been astoundingly sexy, more so than when she had touched his lips earlier. She felt scorched; he appeared cool and composed.

Which meant even considering his proposal would be engaging in a form of lunacy she couldn't afford!

She didn't wait for him to finish with his shoes, but went up the rickety stairs in front of him, though she soon realized putting back on her own shoes had been a mistake, the heels finding every crack between the boards to slide down between. She was with one of the most elegant, composed, handsome men she had ever met, and she felt like she was in the starring role of *March of the Penguins*.

On the seaside of the boardwalk she was passing a scattering of small shingle-sided beachfront homes and cottages. Ethan caught up to her.

She slipped up the first side street of St. John's Cove, where it met the boardwalk, and now less wobbly on the paved walkway, marched up the hill past the old saltbox fishing cottages, one of which she had grown up in and where her brother Mitch still lived. The lobster traps in the front yard were real, not for decoration. He must have brought them home to repair them.

The side street emptied onto the town square, and she crossed the deserted park at the center of the square and went past the statue of Colton's great-grandfather. His great-grandfather looked amazingly like Colton—tall, handsome, powerful—but he had a stuffy look on his face that she had never seen on Colton's. The walkway that bisected the park led straight to Main Street, St. John's Cove.

The colorful awnings over the buildings had been all rolled up, the tables and umbrellas in front of the Clam Digger put away for the night. The street-lights, modeled after old gaslights, threw golden light over the wonderful old buildings, Colonial salt-boxes, shingle-sided, some weathered gray, some stained rich brown.

All the window, door, corner and roof trim was painted white, and old hinged store signs hung from wrought-iron arms above the doors. Each store had bright flower planters in front, spilling over with abundant colorful waves of cascading petunias.

St. John's Cove Main Street was picturesque and delightful—bookstores, antique shops, art galleries and cafés, the bank anchoring one end of the street, the post office the other.

And right in the middle of that was her store, Groom to Grow.

With the Building for Sale sign, that she had managed not to think about for nearly twelve whole hours, swinging gently in front of it. And if that wasn't bad enough, she could see the nose of Amanda's yellow convertible parked at a bad angle beside the staircase that ran up the side of her building to her apartment above the storefront.

Well, where else was Amanda going to go? She had given up her own apartment in anticipation of spending the rest of her life with Charlie, starting tonight.

"Well, this is home."

"This is *your* business?"

She turned at the surprised note in his voice. "Yes. I live in the apartment above it."

He put his hands in his pockets, rocked back on his heels. "That's a strange coincidence. I looked at it today."

"To buy it?" she asked, not succeeding at keeping the waver of fear out of her voice. So far, because of the economy, there had been very little interest in the building.

He shrugged, watching her closely. "I'd only pick it up if I bought the other property, as well. The price is reasonable, probably because the building needs a lot of work. Cape Cod is always a good investment."

"Oh." She tried to sound unconcerned, but knew she failed miserably. "What would you do with it, if you bought it?"

"Probably do some much needed maintenance on it, and then rent it out. Just think," he teased, "I could be your landlord."

"I doubt that. The rent is a song right now. Once the roof didn't leak and the hot water tap actually dispensed hot water, it would probably be a different story. I can't pay any higher. Once the building sells, I'll probably be looking for a new home. I was counting my lucky stars that there hasn't been much interest in it since it went on the market."

She wished she hadn't admitted that. The Hall

family was notorious for keeping their business to themselves, but she knew Ethan had registered the slight waver in her voice. She pointed her chin proudly to make up for it.

She wished she could afford to buy the building, but she couldn't. Her brothers would probably help her if she asked them, but she knew the lobster business was a tough one. The Hall brothers had invested in a new vessel recently, and she hated to think of putting more stress on their finances.

Her future, and the future of Groom to Grow, were clearly up in the air.

"Hmm," Ethan said easily, teasingly, "maybe I've found just the lure to get you to agree to be my wife."

As if he wasn't lure enough, damn him!

She wasn't in the mood to kid about Groom to Grow and her future. She had parlayed her love of animals into this business and if it wasn't *exactly* what she had planned for her life, at least it allowed her to live in the town she loved, surrounded by the people she cared about.

"Tell me the details of your *proposal*," she said reluctantly.

"When my lawyer made some initial inquiries about the property for sale up the coast, the couple informed him they were *interviewing* potential buyers. They're old people. They have a sentimental attachment to the place. They want to see another

family in there. They've been *interviewing* buyers
and turning them down for two years."

"That's kind of sweet, isn't it?"

He groaned. "Sweet? It's sentimental hogwash.
What does that have to do with business?

"They could sell it to what they think is the perfect
family, and that family could turn around and sell it
in a year or two, disillusioned with life at Cape Cod."

He was being very convincing, and she knew that
happened all the time. The *sumpies* were fickle in
their love of Cape Cod.

They came and bought cottages and properties here
during those perfect months of summer. Then they
discovered they hated the commute. Or that outfitting
and running two households was not very relaxing.
That there were really only two or three true months
of summer to enjoy their expensive real estate. Spring
and fall were generally cold and blustery; winter in
St. John's Cove was not for the faint of heart.

"So," Sam said uneasily, "you want me to pretend
to be your wife for one day. To go dupe those old
people out of their property."

He didn't just play with money—he played
with people.

"I don't see it like that," he said evenly. "It's
business. It's unrealistic of them to think they're
going to control what happens to the property after
they sell it."

He was right in a pragmatic way. If she could be

as businesslike as he was maybe the future of Groom to Grow wouldn't be so uncertain. She made a decent living at what she did, she loved it and it allowed her to stay in St. John's Cove. But it had never taken off to the point where she could sock away enough money to buy her own property.

"I said I'd make it worth your while."

So, here was the truth about him. She should have known it the first time she had looked into those devil-dark eyes. Ethan Ballard was Lucifer, about to hold out the one temptation she couldn't refuse, the future of Groom to Grow. Though her eyes slid to his lips when she thought that, and she realized he might have two temptations she would have trouble walking away from.

"If the deal goes the way I want it to, I'll buy this building, and you can rent the space from me. I'll guarantee you the same terms you have now for at least a year, since you'd be putting up with some noisy and inconvenient repairs."

Sam, of all people, knew life didn't have guarantees, but a reprieve from that For Sale sign almost made her weak in the knees.

"You want that place badly," she said, trying not to act as shocked as she felt.

"Maybe. The initial assessments look very promising."

"Enough for you to throw in a *building*?" she asked cynically.

He shrugged. "So, I end up with the beachfront house *and* some of St. John's Cove Main Street. The price on this building was very fair. Sounds win-win to me."

"And if the deal doesn't go the way you want?"

"How could it not?" he said smoothly. "With you as my wife?"

In other words, if she played the role well, things would go exactly as he wanted them to. She had a feeling things in Ethan Ballard's life went his way.

"If, despite my best efforts to play your devoted wife, they don't sell you their property?" she pressed. "What then?"

"The deal is off. I'd be heading up a development team to work on the other property—carpenters, plumbers, electricians, roofers—so it would be no big deal to send them over to do some work on this building while we're here. But it wouldn't make good business sense to send them in for this building alone. I'm hands-on. If I can't be here to supervise, I'm not doing it."

"Oh."

"Take a chance," he said in his best charm-of-the-devil voice. "You won't be any further behind if things don't work out. Besides, it might be fun."

Oh, sure. Of course it was fun to dance with the devil, but there was always a price to be paid.

"I have to think about it," she said, deducing he was a man far too accustomed to getting his own way.

She certainly didn't want him to see how easily she was swayed by his charm, or how much she wanted what he was offering. He didn't have to know she was already ninety percent at yes.

Though in truth more than fifty percent of that *yes* was that she was reluctantly intrigued by him, even if she was uneasy about the deal.

A light turned on in her apartment.

They both turned and looked up at the lighted window. Amanda, still in her bridal gown, was pacing in front of the window.

I'm getting a stomachache, Sam noted to herself. Out loud, she said coolly, "It was nice meeting you. Thanks for walking me home."

"I'll drop by in the morning, around nine. I'll pick you up right here, outside, so it's not awkward if you decide against it. If you're here, great, and if you're not, I'll assume you didn't want to come. No problem." He looked at her for a long moment, and she could feel herself holding her breath. He was debating kissing her! She knew it. And she didn't know if she was relieved or regretful when he walked away!

By nine the next morning, the other ten percent had swung over to Ethan Ballard's side. The truth was, Sam would have thrown in with Genghis Khan to get away from the intensity of emotion that had swept into her life with the runaway bride. Sam had spent most of the night trying to console her friend, who was inconsolable, but who wouldn't tell her what horrible crime Charlie had committed this time.

Despite her cynicism about love and marriage, Sam would have done anything to make Charlie and Amanda's relationship work, to see her friends happy. Her sense of powerlessness in the face of Amanda's distress made her eager to escape.

Still, even though she was waiting at the curb for Ethan Ballard, Sam was determined he wasn't going to have it all his way.

No, the girl Ethan had proposed to last night was banished. Gone was the makeup and the hair, gone was the suggestive dress.

Sam's face was scrubbed clean, her hair loose but covered with her favorite ball cap. She was wearing an old pair of faded khakis, and a T-shirt that belonged to her brother Bryce. She had an uglier one that belonged to Mitch, but Amanda was shuffling around the apartment in it this morning since everything Amanda owned was at Charlie's house.

Still, Sam was satisfied that she certainly would not be what anyone would picture as the wife of Mr. Ethan Ballard.

And she had the new dog, Waldo, with her, too. People dropped off strays with her, counting on her to work her magic with them and then to find them good homes. Sam had never said no to a dog who needed a place to go.

This dog was particularly sensitive to emotion,

and when Amanda had become so overwrought that she was puking, he had started sympathy-puking right along with her.

Sam and the dog were actually sitting on the curb when Ethan drove up the street slowly in a gorgeous newer-model luxury car. Waldo, half Chinese pug and half mystery, was dressed in an army camo hoodie since the morning fog had not quite lifted, and the breeze coming off the ocean was sharp. Sam could not stop herself from spoiling the dogs and cats that had temporary refuge with her.

Sam saw the look on Ethan Ballard's face when he saw her sitting by the curb with her mutt. She thought about the mission they were about to embark on and had the uncharitable hope that the dog would puke in his luxurious car.

If Ethan even stopped to pick them up! Maybe he would take one look at the real Samantha Hall and drive right on by!

CHAPTER THREE

ETHAN BALLARD drove down Main Street of St. John's Cove, enjoying the Sunday morning quiet of it, but aware that despite his words last night—*If you're here, great, and if you're not, I'll assume you didn't want to come*—he hadn't meant the *no problem* follow-up. For some reason, he *wanted* her to come with him.

And not necessarily because of the Finkles, either. Last night, after he had left Samantha Hall and walked back down the beach alone, he had thought of her comment about *duping those old people out of their property,* and not liked that very much.

Usually Ethan regarded business as a large chess game. He liked *winning.* He had turned his competitive nature to that and found it far more fulfilling and less full of pitfalls than relationships. But when had he become so focused on the win that he was willing to *dupe* people?

Maybe it would be just as well if Samantha didn't

show up this morning. He'd drive up the coast, present the Finkles with a very good offer, take it or leave it, no games, no *duping*.

So, if it would be just as well if she didn't show up, and if he was a man who avoided the pitfalls of relationships and had made business, pragmatic and predictable, a safe harbor from *emotion,* then it was probably not a good thing that he felt dismayed that Samantha was not waiting for him.

A little boy in a ball cap and a scruffy dog sat on the curb. Ethan slowed, looked past them, to see if Samantha was coming down her staircase. She wasn't, and aware of a sharp pang of disappointment, he debated going and knocking on her door.

But that hadn't been the agreement, and if the yellow convertible was any indication, his cousin, Amanda, was still there. His brow furrowed as he thought of his young, lovely cousin starting the day yesterday so full of hope, and now being so distressed. Should he go say something to her? Or would his own discomfort with all things emotional just make everything worse?

While he mulled over his options, the little boy stood up, and the dog yapped its dislike. Ethan glanced at the pair again.

And slammed on the brakes. His eyes widened.

That was Samantha Hall? Oh, it was her all right, those wide-set gray-green eyes in the shadow of the ball cap, the delicate features, the sensuous curve of her mouth. But all those delectable curves that dress had shown off last night were disguised this morning.

Ethan leaned over and opened the door for her, surprised by how he felt. Intrigued. And he had the same feeling he'd had last night after talking to her brother. That what Samantha needed more than anything else was for someone to see right past the ball cap, and the men's T-shirt, to the woman in her.

The woman he had tasted when his lips had brushed hers so briefly.

The woman he had touched when she had stumbled putting on her shoe, felt the pure and feminine sensuous energy of her.

"Good morning," he said as she slid into the seat beside him. "I nearly drove by. I didn't recognize you."

"This is the *real* me," she said defensively, settling the dog on her lap.

Is it? he wondered. Her dog glared at him and growled. She appeared to have taken more time dressing the dog than herself.

"I thought maybe that was how you felt Mrs. Ethan Ballard would look," he said mildly, and glancing up at the apartment window asked, "Do you think I should go say something to Amanda?"

"She's finally sleeping."

He heard the concern in Samantha's voice, and felt, ridiculously, as if he was the white knight riding in, not to rescue his cousin, but Samantha.

"You look a little the worse for wear this

morning," he said, checking over his shoulder as he pulled away from the curb.

"I don't have the wardrobe to look like Mrs. Ethan Ballard," she said proudly. "Unless I wore the dress from last night and it didn't seem appropriate for daywear."

"I wasn't referring to your clothes," he said dryly. "You just look tired."

"Oh."

"What do you think Mrs. Ethan Ballard's wardrobe would look like?"

She slid him a sideways look. "I guess that depends what kind of woman you go for. I wonder. Trashy? Or classy. I'm going to guess classy."

"Thanks," he said dryly. "I think."

Classy. He thought of Bethany, with her pedigree and her designer wardrobe, her tasteful jewelry, her exotic, expensive scents. Classy, but when he'd scraped the surface, challenged her, she'd been superficial as hell.

The woman beside him in her baseball cap and khakis, with her innate honesty and decency, seemed a lot more classy than Bethany. If classy meant *genuine.* Real. And somehow at this moment that is what it meant to him.

"Classy it is," he said. The next town, Stone Harbor, was past the turnoff to the Finkles, but since it was just a few minutes away on the winding coast road, and it was bigger than St. John's Cove, a few of its Main Street stores would be open on Sunday. He pulled over in front of a boutique, Sunsational, that looked upscale and *classy*.

Luckily the fog was persisting so it wasn't yet hot enough to worry about leaving the dog in the car, though he rolled all the windows partly down.

He opened the door for Samantha, aware he was enjoying this, aware that his rendezvous with the Finkles was shimmering like an oasis he might never arrive at but he didn't mind because the journey there was proving just as interesting. Make that more interesting.

"What are we doing?" Samantha asked, eyeing the boutique.

"Making you into Mrs. Ballard. The classy version." He grinned. "Though trashy would be more fun."

He saw she looked wounded, and that he had insulted her by insinuating she wouldn't make a great Mrs. Ballard just the way she was.

But he felt he saw a truth about her that she might have been missing herself: that what she was wearing now was a disguise of sorts intended to hide who she really was.

"Look," he said, hastily, "you look fine the way you are. But if I don't end up buying your building, you've given me your time for nothing. Let me do something for you. Consider it a thank-you in advance."

Pride played across her face, but he saw the

faintest wistfulness in the quick glance she cast at the door. He knew it! She had every woman's delight in shopping!

Still, when he held open the door of the store for her and she marched by him, she was scowling.

He touched the place where her brow was knit. "Have fun!" he instructed her.

She looked at him, glanced around the store. He could clearly see she was struggling with a decision, and he was relieved when something in her relaxed.

"Okay," she said, and gave him a small, careful smile. It occurred to him that that smile changed everything, changed far more than a dress ever could. He saw the radiance in her, and realized the sighting was precious, the part of herself, along with her femininity, that she kept hidden.

It was a treasure he felt drawn to find.

Still, her idea of *fun* turned out to be a menace, because she gave him the *trashy* version of Mrs. Ballard. She flounced out of the dressing room in a too short white leather skirt and a hot-pink halter top, flipped a dark wave of luscious hair over her naked shoulder and watched his reaction solemnly.

The truth was he was flummoxed. She looked *awful*. And yet his mouth went absolutely dry at the slender temptation of her perfect curves, her toned and tanned legs, the glimpse of her belly button where the top didn't quite meet the skirt.

When he struggled for words, and all that came

out was an uncertain *Ah,* the solemn look faded
from her face and she laughed. She was kidding
him, paying him back.

But when she laughed her whole face lit up and
her eyes danced with mischief, and he knew he'd
glimpsed the treasure he'd been looking for. The real
Samantha Hall, despite the costume she had put on.

A half hour later and a half dozen more sedate
outfits later, she emerged from the dressing room
and twirled in front of him. The defensiveness had
left her, and he was delighted at how thoroughly she
was enjoying herself. From the sassiness of her pose,
she knew it was the perfect outfit, and so did he.

She wore a summer skirt, of light silk, an amazing
blend of seaside colors, the turquoise of the sea and
the pale blue of the sky. She had paired it with casual
sandals that showed the delicate lines of her feet, and
he remembered the white-hot feeling of holding that
tiny foot in the palm of his hand last night.

When she twirled, her loose, glossy hair fanned
out and the skirt flew around her, revealing, again,
those amazing legs, and hinting at her gypsy spirit.

She had on a cream linen jacket, that she hadn't
done up, and under it was a camisole so simple
there should be no reason that it made his mouth go
as dry as the more flamboyant pink halter top she
had tried on first.

"What do you think?" she asked.

He thought she was the perfect Mrs. Ballard. He

*thought he had dragged her in here to show her
something of herself, and had seen something of
himself instead. That he was vulnerable to her.*

"You look perfect," he said gruffly, and then tried
to short-circuit his own vulnerability, to make her
stop looking at him like *that,* in a way that made his
heart feel like it would swoop out of his chest and land
in the palms of her hands. "Let's go dupe the Finkles."

The happy look faded from her face, and he was
sorry even though he knew it was better for both of
them if they didn't forget what this was all about.

"This is the one," she said, suddenly cool.
"Let's go."

He mourned the loss of the magic of the moments
they had just shared, even as he knew they made
things way too complicated.

At the front desk, Samantha went outside while
he paid. The clerk offered to package up the old
clothes for him, but he just shook his head. Even if
she was mad at him, he never wanted to see her in
those clothes—that particular lie—again.

She didn't ask about her clothes when he joined
her. Her eyes were challenging him to back down,
to say the subterfuge had gone far enough.

But the look of disdain in her eyes was so much
safer for him than the look in her eyes when she had
been twirling in front of him, filled with glorious certainty of herself, that he felt more committed than
ever to his plan. They'd visit the Finkles, he'd take

her home. Leave her with the outfit to assuage some faint guilt he was feeling. If he did end up buying her building, he would keep it strictly business.

Though he wasn't sure how, since he had utterly failed to keep things strictly business so far.

What if it could be real?

He didn't even know her, he scoffed at himself. But when he looked at her, her eyes distant, her chin pointed upward with stubbornness and pride, he felt like he did know her. Or wanted to.

"What's the plan now?" she said.

"We'll go to the Finkles. Let's just say we're engaged instead of married," he told her.

The stiff look of pride left her face and something crumpled in her eyes. "Even dressed up, I'm not good enough, am I?"

"No!" he said, stunned at her conclusion. "That's not it at all. The problem is you are way too good for me. Duper of old people, remember?"

And then he hurriedly opened the car door and held it for her, before he gave into the temptation to take her in his arms and erase any thought she'd ever had about not being good enough, before he gave in to the temptation to kiss her until she had not a doubt left about who she really was, a *woman,* who deserved more than she had ever asked of the world.

He knew if he was smart, he would just pass the turnoff he was looking for and take her straight back to St. John's Cove, cut his losses.

But now he felt he had to *prove* to her it was him that was unworthy, not her.

It was probably the stupidest thing he'd ever done, to continue this charade.

But looking back over the events of the last day, since he had first seen Samantha Hall standing at the altar beside his cousin, it seemed to Ethan Ballard he had not made one smart decision. Not one.

He glanced at the woman sitting with her dog slobbering all over her new silk skirt, trying to read her expression.

"Look," he said awkwardly, "any man would be lucky to call you his wife. And that was before we went shopping." He was a little shocked by how much he meant that, but he had failed to convince her.

He wanted to just call this whole thing off, forget the Finkles and go home to the mess-free life he took such pride in.

"Humph," she said skeptically.

If he did call it off now, was Samantha really going to think she had failed to measure up to his standard for a wife? He sighed at how complicated this innocent little deceit had become.

Here he was smack-dab in the middle of a mess of his own making.

Samantha Hall looked straight ahead, refusing to meet his eyes, but the dog slid him a contemptuous look and growled low in its throat.

Ethan Ballard thought he had heard somewhere that dogs were excellent judges of character.

"I used to play baseball," he said. It was a measure of his desperation that he was trying to *win* her respect back this way, when he hated it when people liked him for his former career. But the truth was, right about now, Ethan would take her liking any way he could get it.

He *wanted* that look back in her eyes, he wanted the radiance back, even though it was a very dangerous game he played.

"Didn't we all?" she said.

"I meant professionally. I played first base for the Red Sox for a season."

"And you are telling me this why?" Not the tiniest bit of awe in her voice.

"I'm trying to impress you," he admitted sadly, "since I've managed to make such a hash of it so far."

"Humph."

"I'll take that as a fail."

"I grew up with three brothers," she told him, and he could hear the sharp annoyance in her voice. "Every single special occasion of my entire life has been spoiled by their obsession with sports. You know where my brothers were the night I graduated from high school?"

"I'm afraid to ask."

"In Boston."

"Oh, boy," he muttered. "Red Sox?"

She nodded curtly and went back to looking out the window.

It occurred to him he really had stumbled onto the perfect woman for him, a woman capable of not being impressed with what he'd done, who could look straight through that to who he really was.

Not that he'd exactly done a great job of showing her that. Maybe he'd even lost who he really was somewhere along the way, in the pursuit of ambition and success.

And maybe she was the kind of woman who could lead him back to it. If he was crazy enough to tangle with her any longer than he absolutely had to.

With relief he saw the sign he'd been looking for—Annie's Retreat—and he pulled off the main road onto a rutted track.

The first thing that would need work, and a lot of it, was the road, he thought, and it was such a blessed relief to be able to think of that rather than the stillness of the woman beside him.

Life was just plain mean, Sam thought, getting out of the car after the long, jolting ride down a rough road. Waldo bounced out with her. He had snagged her skirt, so she had managed to look upscale for all of fifteen minutes.

Ethan, of course, looked like he was modeling for the summer issue of *GQ,* in dun-colored safari shorts that looked like he had taken a few minutes to press them before he left his hotel this morning. Ditto for the shirt, a short-sleeved mossy-green cotton, with a subtle Ballard Holdings embroidered in a deeper shade of green over the one buttoned pocket.

No wonder she had been downgraded to fiancée! No matter what he said, she was pretty sure it was because she didn't fit in his world.

"Maybe we should leave him in the car," Ethan suggested carefully, as if she was made of glass.

But she was all done being what Ethan wanted her to be, and Waldo came with her, *especially* if he didn't fit into Ethan's world and Ethan's plans.

"The dog comes," she said, "and if you don't like it, or they don't like it, *tough*."

There. That was more like the real Samantha Hall, not like that woman who had stared back at her from the mirror in Sunsational, sensual, grown-up, mature, *feminine*.

Despite her attempts to harden her emotions, Samantha could not deny Annie's Retreat was a place out of a dream she had, a dream that she had been able to keep a secret even from herself until she saw this place. These large properties were almost impossible to come by anymore on this coastline.

It made her remember that once upon a time she had dreamed of turning her love of all things animal into an animal refuge, where she could rescue and rehabilitate animals. Given her nonexistent budget, Groom to Grow had been more realistic, and she still ended up caring for the odd stray, like Waldo, that people brought in. But looking at this property she felt that old longing swell up in her.

The road ended in a yard surrounded by a picket fence, the white paint long since given way to the assaults of the salt air. Early-season roses were going crazy over an arbor; beyond it she could see the cottage: saltbox, weathered gray shake siding, white trim in about the same shape as the paint on the fence.

An attempt at a garden had long since gone wild, and yet it charmed anyway: daises, phlox, hollyhock, sewn among scraggly lawn, beach grass and sand.

A path of broken stones wound a crooked course to the house, where red geraniums bloomed in peeling window boxes. The path ended at an old screen door; the red storm door to the cottage was open through it. Sam could look in the door: a dark hallway burst open into a living room where a wall of salt-stained windows faced an unparalleled view of a restless, gray-capped sea.

She was here to look at a cottage out of a dream, a cottage she would never own. She was here with a man out of a dream, a man who was as unattainable for her as the cottage. *No matter what he said about her being good enough and trying to impress her. Ha-ha.*

Waldo jumped up on the door, put his paws on the screen, sniffed and let out a joyous howl. A small dog came roaring down the hall, skittered on a rug, righted itself and rammed the door. She was out and after a brief sniff, the two dogs raced around the yard, obviously in the throes of love.

If only it was that easy for people, Sam thought. Though she could fall in love with the man beside her in about half a blink if she allowed herself to.

Not that she would ever be that foolish!

A tiny gnome of a woman came to the door, smiled at them from under a thick fringe of snow-white hair. She opened the door to them, glancing at the dogs with tolerance.

Then she looked at them with disconcerting directness, her smile widened and she stuck out her hand. "Annie Finkle."

Ethan took it, introduced himself, then hesitated before he said, "And this is my, er, fiancée, Samantha Hall."

Samantha glanced at him. He was either a terrible liar, or after downgrading her from the wife position, didn't even want her to be his fiancée!

She decided, evil or not, to make him pay for that. She looped her arm around his waist, ran her hand casually and possessively along his back, just as she had seen in-love couples do. The way her life was going this might be as close as she would ever get, so she was going to enjoy every minute of it.

And enjoy it even more because it made him so uncomfortable.

"Darling," she breathed, following Annie into the

living room, not letting go of her hold on him, "isn't this the most adorable house you've ever seen?"

"Adorable," he croaked, and she looked at him and enjoyed the strain she saw in his face. He tried to lift her arm away from him, but she clamped down tighter.

It was a delightful room, completely without pretension. It had dark plank flooring that had never been refinished, and a huge fireplace, the face of it soot-darkened from use. Worn, much used couches faced each other between the huge window and the fireplace. The entire room cried *home*.

"I love the floor coverings," Sam said. "They're unbelievable."

Annie beamed at her. "I hand-paint historic patterns on oilskins. I make more of them than I can use, unfortunately. Artie would like me to open a shop, but I'm probably too old." But even as she said it, she looked wistful. She brought herself back to the moment. "This is my favorite room in the house."

"I love it, too," Sam breathed. "I can just see myself sitting in that rocking chair in the winter, a fire in the hearth, watching a storm-tossed sea." Then she realized it didn't feel like a game, so she upped the ante to remind herself this was fantasy. "Maybe," she cooed, "there would be a baby at my breast."

Something darkened in his already too dark eyes. The set of his mouth looked downright grim as he looked at her. She knew she was playing way out of her league, and she didn't mean baseball, but she stroked his back again, even though it made her stomach drop and her fingers tingle.

She should have known not to even try to get the best of him, because he leaned close to her, inhaled the scent of her hair and then blew his breath into her ear.

"Stop it," he growled in a low tone, and then he gently nipped her ear, just to let her know if she wanted to play hardball he had plenty of experience.

The tingle Sam had been experiencing in her fingers moved to her toes. And back up again.

"Oh," Annie said. "Babies! And you'd come in the winter?"

"If I owned this place," Sam said, "I doubt I'd ever leave it." No, she could see herself here as if it would be the perfect next stage of her life, not the place of change that she had feared, at all.

She could see all her friends gathering here, the Group of Six not disappearing, but expanding as they acquired mates and children, the circle growing in love and warmth. She could sense those unborn children, see them screeching and running on the beach, toasting marshmallows on bonfires at night, falling asleep in parents' arms.

This house cast a spell on Sam that made it so easy to see her brothers, settling down at last, coming here with their wives and children, raising another generation who loved Cape Cod year-round.

This was the kind of place where friends and

family gathered around the fire on deepest winter nights. Where they played rowdy card games and hysterical rounds of charades, enjoying sanctuary in the love and laughter of friends from the bitter winter storms.

Why was it, it was so easy to imagine Ethan, an outsider to that circle, as being at the very center of it? Why is it she knew that he would slide into the circle without creating a ripple, as if he had belonged there always?

Was it the place that created this sensation of belonging? A longing for things that weren't yet, but that she could sense on the horizon?

She realized she was imagining a life that had been once, already. She was believing in something that had died for her when her parents had died.

"I would never leave," she whispered, and then closed her eyes, remembering what that sense of family and community had been like, and feeling deeply grateful that the love of the Group of Six had kept hope alive inside of her even while she denied it.

She opened her eyes when she realized the room was too quiet, and she feared she had inadvertently revealed too much of herself to Ethan Ballard. She scanned the handsome lines of his face and did not like the quizzical expression as he looked at her, as if he knew she had momentarily forgotten it was a game. She forced herself to explore the curve of his lower back with her fingertips again, to distract him, and herself, from what had just happened.

This time, instead of trying to move away from her, Ethan looked at her hard, and saw way too much. Instead of moving away from her touch, he pulled her closer into his side, so that she could feel the steely length of him...and the strong, steady beat of his heart.

It was a terrible sensation, because it felt to Sam as if he was a man you could rely on when you were tired of being alone and afraid of being lonely, a man you could rely on when you decided, finally, you just wanted to go home.

Annie led them through the dining area to the kitchen. It was small, cramped and dated, but Sam thought it was the coziest kitchen she had ever seen, with its bright yellow paint, white curtains blowing in the breeze from an open window.

She tried to get back into the spirit of pretense by saying, "Oh, I can just imagine baking cookies for you here, darling," but in her own ears her voice sounded forced and faraway.

Because she could imagine using this kitchen, even though she had never baked a cookie in her life. It still could become the cheerful hub for all the activity she had imagined moments ago.

"I can hardly wait," he growled, and then kissed her on the tip of her nose, a playful gesture that seemed all too tender and all too real. It should have been a warning to stop before she had embedded herself further in the quicksand of the heart. But instead, it only egged her on, even though she wanted to quit doing this. Not to him, but to herself.

Down the narrow hall they went, the narrowness forcing her to let go of him.

But she made up for it.

The back bedroom was tiny and dark.

"This is the room I want for the nursery," she declared, but unfortunately, as she said it, she could see it, just as she had so clearly seen the future in those other rooms.

And shockingly, so could he.

"I'd knock out this wall," he said, pensively, "and put in a bigger window, a bay one, with a window seat. We could sit here with the baby, together, in the evenings."

The picture that conjured up for her stole her breath. She could so easily imagine him in that tender scene. And that picture stole her drive to make him uncomfortable, to make him pay for this farce. She was done pretending. What it was doing to her heart was far too dangerous.

She did not renew her possessive encircling of his waist, and made no comment about how romantic the master bedroom was, though it had another fire-place in it, and a window that faced the sea.

He also became more and more silent, and Sam wondered if he was looking at the house through a developer's eyes. If he was, she deduced, a bit sadly, there was probably nothing to be saved.

After a tour of the interior of the house they moved outside. Annie's husband, Artie, was in the garden, and they met him, and then Annie laid tea out for all of them on a worn outdoor table that faced the sea.

The dogs had worn themselves out and flopped down, panting under the table. Waldo nuzzled Annie's hand.

"What an adorable dog," the old woman said gently.

"He's looking for a home!" Sam said, never missing an opportunity to place one of her charges.

"I can barely keep up with the one I have," Annie confessed ruefully. "I do love his outfit. Where did you get that?"

"Groom to Grow in St. John's Cove," Sam said. "I—"

Ethan nudged her gently in the ribs, reminding her she was beginning to complicate things by mixing up her fiction with her facts. So instead of saying she owned it, she said, hearing the slight sullenness in her own voice, "I love shopping there."

"I'm going to get a jacket just like that one for Josie!" Annie declared, and Sam thought what a perfect home this would be for Waldo, even as she remembered what she hated about lies. They never stopped. Now this woman was going to show up at her shop in St. John's. What if she inquired about her fiancé? What if people were listening?

Annie's eyes met hers over the tea. "I can see you here," she said quietly to Sam. "I'm so delighted. Finally I can see someone here."

Artie looked at his wife and smiled, and something passed between them that was so sweet and so genuine that it nearly broke Sam's heart in two. No wonder she could feel love in this house, no wonder the place conjured visions of domestic bliss.

"We don't want to sell to just anybody," Artie said. "Annie's a bit fey. She said she'd know when the right people came along. People who would love this ramshackle old wreck of a place as much as we have."

Sam wanted to sink under the table she felt so dreadful. If Ethan got his hands on this old cottage what would he do with it? Tear it down? She saw Ethan leaning forward. Clearly this was the moment he lived for, closing the deal. He probably had papers they could sign in the car.

And suddenly, she just couldn't do it, not even if her whole future and the future of Groom to Grow was at stake.

"Oh," she said, forcing brightness, "we aren't rushing into anything, are we, darling? I'm just not sure if this is the right place for us. There's only three bedrooms, and we are planning a large family. Ethan wants at least six children."

"Six," Annie said with surprise, though it was approving surprise.

"Of course, we could put on an addition," Ethan

said, the smile belying what she interpreted as a warning look in his eyes as he gazed at her.

She ignored the warning. "Darling! You know I have to be sure. You know what they say, don't you?"

"No, I don't," he said tightly.

"If Mama ain't happy, ain't nobody happy," she sang to him, wagging a stern finger below his nose.

He glared at her while the Finkles laughed with delight.

"I think you're right not to rush into anything," Annie said. "Even though the place is getting to be too much for us—look at the flower beds and the paint, disgraceful—we're in no hurry to sell. I'd feel better if I found exactly the right place for us to move on to first."

"Very wise," Sam murmured, not daring to look at the man beside her.

"We're thinking a condo, but I haven't seen one I like yet. They're all so—"

"Generic," Sam provided. She, too, had looked at condos before finding her own charming apartment, with the storefront beneath it, so suited to her needs.

The one she was about to throw away. Because she couldn't do this. Not if Ethan promised to buy the whole of Main Street, St. John's Cove. She *liked* these people and hated herself for being a part of this pretense. Samantha's business meant a lot to her, the world to her, in fact, but she realized she wasn't prepared to sell her soul for it!

"Exactly," Annie said. "Plus, so many of them seem to be prisons for old people. I don't want to retreat from the world. That's part of what bothers me here. Since we retired and spend so much time here, it seems too isolated. I want to be *part* of the community. Maybe have a little rug shop, where I could meet people every day."

"Well, I guess we all need to think about it for a bit," Sam said, nearly choking on her cheer. She finished her tea in a gulp that was very un-Mrs. Ballard-like and got up from the table. "It was so nice meeting you, Annie. Artie. Darling."

But it was Waldo, getting used to being called *darling* who fell in beside her as she went up the crooked walk beside the cottage to the car. She didn't even glance back over her shoulder at the house of her dreams.

Or to see if Ethan Ballard, pretend fiancé, had followed her.

CHAPTER FOUR

"SORRY," Samantha murmured.

"Don't give it a thought."

He was surprised that he meant it. Ethan Ballard should have been furious. The Finkles had been ready to do some preliminary talking about the property, which was everything he'd hoped for and more. Even the cottage, which he had thought from the Internet pictures would be only worth knocking down, had lots of potential.

He told himself people loved the old saltboxes, and he could knock down interior walls to create a more open space, add windows, expand the house toward the rear. But even as he tried to convince himself that, he wondered if part of how charmed Samantha had been with the old place had rubbed off on him. There was no way she was a good enough actress to have pulled off the enraptured look on her face, the light in her eyes, as she had moved from room to room.

But it was probably all a moot point now. He might never get a chance because the little minx sitting beside him, stroking her dog furiously, had done her best to nix the deal.

But he was aware he did not feel furious with Samantha.

More like *cautious* of her. He had felt something stir in him when she had touched him so possessively, and felt it stir again at an even more powerful and primal level when she had talked about sitting in that living room with a baby at her breast.

Even though she'd clearly been trying to get his goat, the picture had taken on a life of its own inside his mind, and somehow the baby she held had been his.

That, even though he was a man who had never given one single thought to having kids, or to domestic bliss. When he'd been engaged to Bethany he'd been too young to think that far ahead. Bethany had never said a single word about children. He'd been her ticket to *Lifestyles of the Rich and Famous,* not a ruined figure and responsibility.

But there was something about Samantha Hall that made a man not just think of those things, but yearn after them.

Plus, at tea with the Finkles, when Samantha had stunned him by declaring they needed time to think about it, Ethan felt as if he had discovered something more valuable than the property.

The woman beside him appeared to be a person incapable of subterfuge, incapable of deceit. How many people were there in the world who would be so true to themselves? He could tell how badly Sam wanted to stay in her store, but she had been unwilling to lie to do it.

But, he reminded himself, there was an irony here. She did lie to herself, the clothes he had disposed of this morning being a perfect example.

Now as they pulled away from Annie's Retreat, he could tell she was relieved the playacting was over.

"I hated that," she said.

"I should never have asked you to do that," he replied. "It was an impulse. I regret it. " But even as he said it, he knew his regret was not one hundred percent. He thought of her fingers on his back, as she teased him, played with him; he thought of nipping the delicate lobe of her ear.

And was aware he wouldn't have missed that for the world.

She misunderstood him. "I know. You could have asked a thousand girls who could have pulled that off better than me. But Annie and Artie were just such nice people. I hated that they wanted us to have that property when it was all a lie."

He said nothing, digesting what she was telling him about herself.

"So, are you done?" she asked. "You aren't going to try to buy it?"

"I'll back off for the time being. What did you think of the property?"

She was silent, as if she did not want to give anything of herself away to him. Not that he could blame her. But he had already seen things, and she seemed to know it was too late to hide them.

"I loved it," she admitted reluctantly.

"So did I."

"But I loved it just the way it was. I mean a few things needed work, the paint, the flower beds, but it would be a shame to change it. A crime."

"Unless you were going to raise six kids there," he teased her.

She delighted him by blushing. "Just trying to play the part."

"Don't give up your day job."

"Don't worry, I won't. Unless I get evicted from my building. Then I'll put out my new sign, Wife for Hire."

He chuckled, and her stance toward him softened a bit.

"I did like your idea about the one wall in the, er, back bedroom," she admitted.

For a reason he wasn't about to investigate, he was sorry she hadn't called it the nursery. Which is probably why he changed the subject, tried to get it back to the nice, safe area of business instead of the very gray area of nurseries.

"I'm glad you're not going to buy my building,"

she said thoughtfully, somber. "It sounded great, but it made me uneasy, too. I don't want to feel indebted to you, but it's more. Ethan, being the youngest in a family, the only girl, I think I'm used to the boys bailing me out. I don't want to rely on other people to fix my problems."

He was struck by her simple bravery.

"I didn't keep my end of our bargain," she continued. "You can have the outfit back, too."

"You know," he said quietly and carefully, "there's a fine balance between being independent and being alone. Sometimes it's good to rely on others, to share your burdens."

He remembered the joy that had lit her eyes when she had first twirled in that outfit, and cursed himself for stealing that happiness from her.

"And sometimes it's okay," he continued, "to accept a gift. It's no threat to your independence. I want you to have the outfit."

She shrugged and he suspected the outfit was going to enjoy approximately the same fate as the flowers she had caught just last night.

Suddenly he wanted out of this mess he had created for himself. Even if he didn't buy Annie's Retreat, he would never be able to shake the vision of this girl twirling in front of the mirror and him, her hair and her skirt giving her a gypsy air, never be able to quite escape the memory of her hand resting on the small of his back, or her quick intake of air when he'd nipped her ear.

In fact, the sooner he put this whole unfortunate lapse in judgment behind him the better. He'd drop her off and wave goodbye. A kiss, even a casual little goodbye peck, was out of the question; the dog would probably bite him if he got that close to her. Besides, it would be one more memory that he had to outrun.

But when he turned onto Main Street, and slowed in front of her store, he could see Charlie Weston was on the sidewalk in front of it. The poor fool, still in his suit from last night, though he'd lost the bow tie, was seated on a stool, with a guitar across his knee, gazing up at the open window of Sam's apartment, oblivious to the astounded, curious looks of passersby.

"Thank goodness it's Sunday. Look what he's done to my sign," Sam said, annoyance and obvious affection mixed in her voice.

Ethan looked at where a ladder was propped against her store sign. The placement of the spindly ladder looked downright dangerous. A clumsy, hand-drawn *S* and *L* had been taped over her sign, turning "Groom to Grow" to "Groom so Low."

"The English language constantly amazes me in its versatility," Ethan said. "Do you think he meant groom so low, as in depressed, or groom solo, as in single?"

"Charlie is not exactly an academic," Sam said affectionately.

"A romantic," Ethan concluded dryly. "Which

would you rather have?" He realized he was truly interested in her answer, but Samantha ignored him, put her window down halfway, looked as if she planned to intervene.

With the car window open it was painfully apparent Charlie was serenading his runaway bride, wailing an old Don Williams song. Charlie's voice was particularly horrible, part whine, part twang, mostly heartbreak and pathos.

Amanda, light of my life—

Ethan glanced at Samantha. She looked like she was going to get out of the car and try to fix this. Her love for her friends showed in the utter distress on her face. But her hand froze on the door handle when something flew out the open window of Samantha's apartment and hit Charlie square in the chest.

"What was that?" Ethan asked, craning his neck to see better. "A rock?"

"One of the little squares of wedding cake that it took Vivian and me four hours to wrap and tie with fuchsia ribbon."

Charlie set down the guitar. "Mandy, come on—"

The window above Charlie snapped shut.

"Now, that's *reality*," Sam said sadly, as if for a while she had believed something else. Ethan thought of the look on her face when she had looked at the cottage.

"*Maannndddyy!*" It was like the bellow of a wounded bull.

The window shot up, and Amanda leaned out. "Go away!"

"I think I better try to talk to them," Samantha said.

Not even for his own self-preservation was Ethan dropping Samantha off in the middle of that. He stepped on the gas.

"What are you doing?" Samantha demanded.

"Rescuing you from *that*. Haven't you heard the expression about not going where angels fear to tread? Lovers' quarrels fall solidly in that category."

"I told you before, I can look after myself." But he didn't miss the fact she looked relieved.

"Well, pretend you can't. Pretend I'm a knight in shining armor and you are a damsel in distress."

"Even if my imagination was that good, I think I've done enough pretending for today."

"Me, too," he said quietly, and was startled by how pleased he was that she looked faintly intrigued. "I'll take you for lunch. Charlie and Amanda should have resolved things by the time we get back."

"I hate to break it to you since you look like the kind of guy who believes in happily-ever-after—" that said sarcastically "—but Amanda and Charlie have been trying to resolve things since they were fourteen."

"A long lunch, then," he said, and was rewarded with her smile, which she quickly doused when he smiled back.

"They are both such good people," she said

softly. "I don't know why it's always so volatile between them."

"Passion," he said. "It's hard stuff to tame." As if he was any kind of expert on passion—or wanted to be thinking about the subject when he was in such close proximity to her!

"I can't leave Waldo in the car. It's getting too hot." To prove her point, she slipped the hoodie off her dog.

He hoped that meant the imminent removal of her own jacket, even as he thought Samantha was showing a remarkable lack of gratitude for his chivalry. He should just turn around and dump her on that sidewalk, but he thought of Charlie wailing, and Amanda throwing things, and her thinking she could do something to fix it, and he just couldn't.

"Okay, we'll buy some sandwiches and eat at the beach."

"I guess I could change into my other clothes."

And deprive him of the camisole? At least he'd made one good decision today, and he admitted it to her now, trying to appear contrite. "Um, I forgot to pick them up after I paid for the new things."

She stared at him, her gaze going right through him. He was never going to be able to tell her a lie. Ever. But what did it mean that he was thinking like that? As if there was an *ever* in their future.

They were having lunch. He was sticking around for another day or two to finish looking at properties in Cape Cod and then he was leaving St. John's

Cove far behind him. And that meant this woman, her dog and his crazy cousin and her heartbroken husband were going to be in his past, not his future.

"You didn't forget," she said, those gray-green eyes narrowing. "You left my clothes on purpose! I'm trying to tell you that's who I really am, jeans and T-shirts, baseball caps."

"And I'm trying to tell you it's not," he said softly but every bit as stubbornly as her.

For a moment she looked ready to fight, but then she just sighed.

"Eating on the beach will probably wreck the skirt," she said. She plucked at something on it.

The material already had a run in it, probably from the dog. She looked up at him suddenly, daring him to draw a conclusion about that.

"Who cares about the damned skirt?" he said, and meant it.

"Now you sound like the *real* me," she said, and when he hooted with laughter, she rewarded him with that smile again, and he was aware of being glad their day together had not ended, and that they had been given a chance to start again.

Ethan Ballard was *rescuing* her, Samantha reminded herself, watching as he stood in line to get hot dogs from Ernie's. And before that, the shopping trip, the visit to Annie's Retreat had all been part of a game. That was how he *played,* pathetic as that was.

None of it was about him liking her.

And why should she like him? He was a bigwig investment shark from Boston who didn't care anything about little people like Annie and Artie and her. He didn't even know how to have a good time.

But she did like him, even knowing how damned foolish that was. She liked him and she was glad in some horrible, fickle part of herself that wasn't sensible that he had asked her to play his bride for a day, even if he had downgraded it to fiancée in the last moment. She was glad she'd gone shopping with him, she was glad to have seen Annie's Retreat and she was glad that he had rescued her from that horrifying scene unfolding outside her store.

Look, she told herself sternly, *you're twenty-five years old. It's hardly a news bulletin that you like a man.*

Well, okay, in this town it probably was, which meant they should go eat their hot dogs somewhere else.

In fact, it was more like *It's about time* than a news flash. What if, for once, she just relaxed into what life offered her instead of trying to fight it?

So, she liked him. How big a deal was it? Why not enjoy that? For one afternoon? Why didn't she teach him what playing really meant, show him a little hint of her world, just as he had shown her a little hint of his?

It didn't mean she had to bring him home to meet

her brothers. It didn't mean they were going to get married and have babies at Annie's Retreat, sweetly intoxicating as those thoughts were.

It just meant she could enjoy the moment, and bring him along for the ride. She didn't have to look at the future, and more important she didn't have to look at the past, and measure everything against the scale of potential loss.

And with that in mind, feeling strangely light, Samantha went down the street from where he was buying hot dogs at Ernie's and bought two kites— the satin fabric kind with the wonderful colors and long, long tails—to fly on the beach after they'd eaten lunch.

As she climbed back into the car, she shucked off the jacket, even though the camisole was probably a little too revealing to wear by itself.

Live dangerously, she ordered herself.

And she was so glad she had obeyed when she saw the heat flash through Ethan's eyes when he got back in the car.

"Nice kites," he said, his voice hoarse.

She should have slugged him. That would have made her brothers proud. But for some reason, tired of living her brothers' vision for her instead of her own, she just laughed.

She took the hot dogs and drinks from his hands, but when she noticed he had gotten water for the dog the unwanted stab of tenderness she felt for him made her wonder if it was going to be possible to keep this simple.

But she told herself it was too late to change her mind, and that there was no such thing as a Hall who was a chicken, and she directed him to a beach that was dog friendly and just far enough from St. John's Cove that she hoped they weren't going to see any locals who would be reporting her impulsive outing to Mitch.

CHAPTER FIVE

THIS is what you got when you made the decision to live dangerously, Sam thought. This is what you got when you decided to show six feet of pure, muscled man how to play.

Ethan had shrugged off his shirt fifteen minutes ago, and now he was running on the hardened pack of the surf, the dog at his heels, unraveling the spool of kite string behind him. His laughter rang out, clear and true, like church bells.

"Run faster," she called to him, holding the kite at the other end of the string, waiting for exactly the right moment to toss it into the waiting breeze.

"I'm running as fast as I can," he protested.

"My granny Hall can run faster than that!"

He rewarded her with a burst of speed, and she admired the clean, powerful lines of his legs for a moment—the purely masculine energy of him—before she took mercy on him and tossed the kite in the air.

"Launch attempt forty-two," she called.

"Ninety-two," he shot back, getting the hang of this playing stuff. The truth was neither of them were really counting the number of times they had tried to get the thing in the sky. This time, the kite caught the wind and wiggled upward, a bright yellow sun with thirty feet of rainbow silk unraveling behind it.

But she couldn't watch the kite for long, gorgeous as it was against a sky that had proved flawless once the fog had lifted. The sea, restless during their visit with the Finkles, had become quiet. Instead she watched the play of his muscles under sun-gold skin, admiring the broadness of shoulders and the tautness of belly, the white flash of his teeth as he tilted his head back to watch the kite.

The smile disappeared as the kite tilted crazily one way, then the other, and then nosedived straight down toward the ocean!

"No!" she cried. "Don't let it get wet."

He managed, at the last moment, to maneuver it away from the water, so it planted itself deeply into the sand.

A lesser man might have groaned in frustration, but he laughed, and began rolling up the string, ready to try again. "Get ready for launch attempt one hundred and six," he instructed her.

"My brothers would like that," she said, picking the kite out of the sand and inspecting the frame for damage, while he rolled string. "You're no quitter."

And then she realized she had spoken the thought out loud, as if he was a candidate to squire their sister, but she realized she was taking herself too seriously when Ethan appeared not to notice the comment at all.

She reminded herself again to just play, to just enjoy the gift of this day. They tried to launch the kite again, and then again.

Ethan tried to bring his fine business mind to the activity: he licked his finger and tried to calculate the strength of the wind, he made adjustments to the frame, he fiddled with the tail. But finally, by magic rather than science, his kite lifted on the wind, took string, pulled upward and stayed.

Then, with one hand holding his kite spool, he had to try to help her get hers in the air. It was his turn to hold the kite, while she ran.

The skirt, thankfully, didn't hinder her running ability. In fact, she liked the way it felt skimming along her legs, flying up around her as she raced down the sand.

"Faster," he yelled at her. "Run faster, gypsy woman."

So, he had noticed the flying skirt, too.

The camisole wasn't built for athletic activity; the straps were as annoying as the ones on the bridesmaid's dress had been last night. She nearly lost the kite every time she had to push a strap back up.

Finally, with her gasping like a fish, her kite

joined his in the sky. The kite zinged upward, taking string like a fish on a run.

"Hey," she yelled at him. "Keep your kite away from me!" If she really meant that, she wouldn't keep moving back down the sand toward him, but she did, until they stood almost shoulder to shoulder, heads craned back as they maneuvered the kites.

Naturally he took her command to stay away from her kite as a challenge, and he kept bringing his kite recklessly close to hers so that they nearly touched, so that they looked like they were dancing with each other, swaying, dipping, falling, soaring.

It was like watching a mating ritual. And the result was about the same, too.

The kites finally collided, the strings tangled and they fell to the sand like a parachute that had not opened properly.

"You call yours Charlie, and I'll call mine Amanda," he said, flopping down on his back in the sand.

Waldo, exhausted from chasing the kites, took up a post beside him, eyeing Ethan with the suspicion of a spinster chaperone, but not growling at him anymore.

Sam flung herself on her back on the sand beside Ethan. The camisole was stuck to her, and her hair was glued to her forehead. The skirt was limp and crushed.

Which was probably how she would feel tomorrow when it sunk in that it was over. But for now, she enjoyed the feeling of his eyes on her, warm with appreciation. She wanted to touch his back again.

It probably felt different naked than it had felt with the shirt on it.

She shoved her renegade hands under her back.

"I'm hot," he said. "I've got to get in the water."

She looked wistfully at the calm sea. "No swimsuit."

"So what? Don't worry about it. We're engaged. Practically. Besides, nobody's watching us."

And then, as if it was taking her too long to make up her mind, he stood and stretched. He was going to go in without her!

Except he wasn't. He took one step toward the water, and then ducked back on her, flipped her over, put one arm behind her back and one behind her knees and heaved her up, the motion seeming effortless on his part.

She was cradled against his chest, so shocked by sensation of his naked, sun-heated skin, that for a whole three seconds she didn't even fight him.

But then, grinning wickedly, he moved toward the water.

Whose dumb idea had it been to teach him how to play? Not letting on—she hoped—how much she was enjoying all this, she struggled, and gave a token scream.

"Don't! The camisole will be see-through if it gets wet! Ethan!"

"I won't look." But he winked to let her know he was just a guy, after all, and he probably would.

Her struggles were no match for his strength, a fact that pleased her way too much considering she had always taken such pride in thinking she could look after herself.

He waded out into the surf, carrying her easily over the first few rollers. Waldo barked frantically on shore, afraid to get his feet wet.

"My hair," she told him, one last attempt to save herself from the embarrassment of the camisole that was going to turn transparent. She blinked at him with every ounce of feminine wiles she possessed.

He wasn't fooled. He laughed. "You don't give a rat's whiskers about your hair."

And then he slipped his arms out from under her. She fell into the water with an ungraceful crash, drank a bit of salt and got water in her eyes. Still, despite those discomforts, the water was cold on her hot skin, invigorating, as sensual as a touch.

She was glad he had taken the decision to get wet out of her hands, not that she intended to let him know that!

She stood up, sputtering, to see him already running away, crashing through the incoming rollers, sending gleeful looks back over his shoulder at her.

She yanked off the skirt, sorry to have it meet such an untimely end, and dove into the breakers after him. In water, she could swim faster than she could run! All Halls were part dolphin, and Sam loved water. She moved into a strong crawl, watched him glance back once more before diving, cleanly slicing a wave with the strength of his body.

He moved out past the breakers, then cut a course parallel to the shore. She was amazed that he swam as well as she did, or any of her brothers. She wasn't even sure she could beat him in a race to the buoys.

The initial cold shock of the water had faded; it felt perfect now, like an embrace, like soft silk against her skin.

"What are you going to do with me when you catch me?" he called, flipping over, treading for a moment, *letting* her close some of the gap between them.

"I'm going to drown you."

"That's what I was afraid of." He let her get to where she could almost touch him, and then with an easy grin he took off again, heading back toward the shore, letting the waves carry him.

He paused again, near shore, finally getting breathless. "Wouldn't it just be easier to admit you're glad you're in the water?"

"Easier for you!"

"You love it out here. Woman, you are part fish! Mermaid."

"Don't try to charm me."

He swam close, treaded water, tried to peer beneath the surface at the camisole she was pretty sure was now transparent. She flattened her palm against the water and splashed him hard in the face.

She should have remembered he was not a

quitter, because instead of dissuading him, he took it as a challenge, swam toward her, ignoring her shouts to stay back, her laughter, her increasingly aggressive splashing.

One final duck, and she was in the circle of his arms, his flesh warm through the veil of the sea. Instead of trying to pull away she surrendered to his easy strength and to the sensation of her wet camisole pressed into the slippery surface of his chest.

His feet found the sandy bottom, and he held her and went still. The playfulness died on his face.

"You're beautiful," he said softly.

"I told you not to try to charm me."

He kissed her.

And she was charmed. Completely.

It wasn't like that brushing of lips she had instigated last night. His lips claimed her, possessed her, asked more of her than she had ever thought she had to give. They stripped her to her soul, and built her back up, showed her, finally, that he had been right all along.

He knew who she really was. Not a girl any longer, content to play a child's games.

She was a woman, and it was a wonderful thing to be.

He tasted of salt. And strength. And promises.

She kissed him back, hungry for him, starving for this thing that was happening between them.

Waldo moaned from shore, a plaintive howl, and it pulled her, ever so slightly, from the place she was.

Enough that she remembered all her brothers' warnings about what men *really* wanted. It was what she really wanted, too, wasn't it?

But somehow it wasn't. Some instinct for survival told her it was way too soon, told her that there would be nothing but regret at the end of this road if she followed it too far.

Regretfully Samantha took advantage of the fact he was distracted—very distracted—placed both her hands on his shoulders, pushed hard enough that he lost his footing and went under the water.

He came up laughing, shaking droplets of water from his face and hair, and then he came after her, and they played it all out again, the kisses never quite as deep, never quite as hungry as that first one.

Finally exhausted and exhilarated they moved out of the water. She managed to snag her skirt, now as attractive as a lump of soggy tissue paper, from the surf. Ethan had left his shirt at the water's edge, and he pulled it quickly around her, but not before his gaze burned her.

They had no towels, so they lay down in the white, fine sand, the sun kissing them back to warmth.

His shoulder touched hers, his eyes stayed on her face, a small appreciative smile on his lips.

"Do you think things have blown over at your place? I could drop you off, you could change clothes. I'll go back to my hotel and change, too. Then we could go grab a bite to eat together."

Together. A small word, used every day, thousands of times a day.

How could it sparkle with new meaning? How could she feel like she didn't want to leave him, not even for as long as it took to change clothes?

It was weak to feel this way. So why did she feel as if she had waited all her life to feel it?

"Dinner," he said. "Somebody told me the Clam Digger is spectacular."

She remembered her last date at the Clam Digger. She wasn't quite ready to expose all the rawness of these new feelings to her watching community—or her overly protective brothers. Not that they had acted very protective last night.

But brothers could be unpredictable, especially Mitch.

"I could grab my little barbecue and we could pick up some steaks and shrimp, barbecue down here on the beach." That felt private. And easier than looking at him over a dinner plate, with strangers all around them.

Or worse, in St. John's Cove, not strangers at all!

"Perfect."

He didn't seem to care about the effects of the sand and the salt water on his car any more than he had cared about the skirt. He helped her in, and they drove back to her apartment.

She was happy to see that the street in front of her place was quiet. The ladder had been moved and the letters taken down, only straggly pieces of tape left where they had been. Unfortunately she could still see the nose of Amanda's yellow convertible.

He saw it, too. "You want me to come in with you? Maybe I could say something helpful."

She was touched that he didn't want to leave her alone to deal with Amanda's heartbreak, but she wasn't sure if Amanda would appreciate his concern or be embarrassed that her very successful cousin was witnessing the breakdown of her life.

"No, it would be better if you didn't."

"Okay. How about if I come back for you in about an hour?"

"Fine."

Not the least self-conscious—this was a resort town after all—Sam took the stairs two at a time, loving the feel of his too large shirt brushing her naked thighs.

She opened the door to her apartment and felt that wonderful sensation of homecoming that she felt every single time she walked through the door.

Her apartment was a treasure. This building was nearly as old as the town, and Sam's apartment had many of the original features, gorgeous hardwood floors, wainscoting, copper roof panels, leaded glass windows, luxurious oak crown moldings and trim.

It had character, she had always thought with pleasure.

Right now it had one extra character.

Amanda was there still in the too large shirt Sam had left her in this morning.

Her friend was a huddle of misery on the couch, bare legs tucked inside the shirt, patting at her tears, her face swollen and blotchy. She was glued to a DVD. *Wedding Crashers*. Beside it were a number of other DVD cases, *The Wedding Singer*, *My Best Friend's Wedding*, *Four Weddings and a Funeral*.

Sam picked up the control and turned off the TV, before putting her arms around her friend. "You've seen some of these a dozen times," she said gently.

"I want to see what real love looks like!"

"These are fantasies, not the greatest source for a reality check. You threw a piece of cake at real love this afternoon."

"I don't think Charlie married me because he loves me," Amanda whispered, forlorn.

"What?" Sam sank down on the couch beside her, but Amanda leaped up and dashed to the washroom. She didn't even get the door shut before she started throwing up.

Waldo, thankfully, was so tired from his big day that he stayed curled up in his bed by the door.

Amanda wandered back in, looking like death.

"Amanda, this has got to stop. You are making yourself sick. Charlie loves you madly. At least talk to him."

"You think I'm sick because I'm upset?" Amanda

asked shrilly, and then bitterly, "I guess he hasn't managed to tell everyone in town yet."

Samantha felt herself go very still. Suddenly she saw Amanda getting sick and the firestorm of emotions in a different light.

"I'm pregnant," Amanda announced joylessly, though Sam had already figured it out. "That's why we rushed everything, why we decided to get married so fast. And then he had to go and tell his mother at the wedding, when he had promised he wouldn't. You know her. She'll tell everybody."

It seemed to Sam everyone would know in fairly short order anyway. "Why the big secret?" she asked carefully.

"Because I don't want everyone in town thinking I got married because I *had* to," Amanda said shakily.

"Amanda, honey, in this day and age no one gets married because they *have* to."

"No, I guess not," she said doubtfully, and laid her head companionably on Sam's shoulder. "He makes me madder than anyone on earth, Sam. Is that love?"

"You're asking me what love is?"

But for some reason she thought of how she had felt at Annie's Retreat earlier today, had that moment of *belief.* She could picture, again, her group of friends there, their young families with them.

And leading the charge would be the oldest of this coming generation, a little boy or girl who would probably look like some delightful combination of Amanda and Charlie.

"I could probably get an annulment," Amanda said, and started crying again.

Sam was no lawyer, but it seemed to her the relationship had been consummated, just not on the wedding night, and that made her uncertain how the whole annulment thing worked. Not that she thought it would be a very good idea to share that with Amanda right now.

Instead she felt again that *sense* she had had in the cottage. Of one stage of life ending, and another beginning, all unfolding seamlessly according to a plan that she might not be able to predict, but that she could trust.

"Everything is going to be all right," Sam said, and she heard the strength and the confidence in her own voice.

"It is?" Amanda asked.

"Yes," she said firmly, "it is."

Amanda lifted her head off her shoulder, regarded her thoughtfully. "There's something different about you."

"Oh," Sam said carelessly, "I've been out in the sun all day. New freckles, salt in my hair. You know."

Apparently Amanda didn't know. "That's not it," she said before asking, her head tilted to one side, smiling, the first smile since she'd run out of the reception, "Whose shirt is that, anyway?" And then she squinted at the fine print that Sam had forgotten was above the pocket.

"Ethan," she whispered, and then she smiled as if the sun had come out.

For a woman disillusioned by the course of true love, Amanda was a hopeless romantic.

Or maybe she wanted to focus on a love story other than her own, her choices in movies being a case in point.

"You and Ethan would be perfect together," she breathed.

"You're being silly," Sam said. "We barely know each other."

But Amanda insisted on acting like they had posted banns at St. Michael's. She hugged Sam hard to her.

"I always knew there would be a perfect guy for you," she whispered. "And I'm so glad it's Ethan."

And then she burst into tears—presumably at her own lack of a perfect guy—all over again.

Or maybe because she was pregnant.

"Look, I don't have to go out tonight," Sam said. "Maybe it would be better if I stayed with you."

"Oh, no," Amanda said. "My mom's coming over in a bit. Before she does, I'll help you get ready."

Unfortunately Amanda, who *had* picked the pink fuchsia, insisted on helping her pick out an outfit for the evening.

And didn't seem to hear her when she said they were barbecuing on the beach.

Looking at herself in the mirror a while later, Sam wasn't quite sure how Amanda had made this outfit materialize from her wardrobe. Her friend had turned a sow's ear into a silk purse. Sam might have tried to stop Amanda's enthusiastic makeover, but Amanda had been so animated, and seemed to be forgetting her own troubles, so she had gone along.

Now what Sam saw made a light go on in her eyes. She looked stunning: shorts ending mid-thigh, underneath a casual short-sleeved beach top that Amanda had totally recreated with the simple addition of a tight belt. Lastly, Amanda had dug up the silk scarf that she had given Sam herself last Christmas, and knotted it casually at her throat.

Then she'd dug into the makeup they had used for the wedding, and again because it was making Amanda so happy, Sam had gone along.

But maybe it wasn't the outfit or the makeup that had put this new light in her eyes, the light that made her look—and feel—as if she was not a little girl, not anyone's little sister anymore.

In the mirror, what looked back at her was one-hundred-percent pure woman. And Sam felt, not a sense of betraying her *real* self, but rather a sense of welcoming a disowned part of herself home.

CHAPTER SIX

ETHAN watched the flames of their fire leap against the black star-studded sky, pulled Samantha deeper into the V of his legs, felt her settle back against his chest. They had just cooked clams in a bucket over the open fire, and now the night was growing a bit chilly.

She was already wearing his shirt over her own. Today, she had been wearing another camisole-style top, misty gray, a delicate concoction that had showed off the fineness of her figure and skin. But what he had noticed most of all was that it made her eyes look more gray than green.

He suspected it was new, and he loved how Sam was, day after day, embracing the feminine side of herself. There was no doubt she liked the reaction an outfit like that got from him, but he saw that she was genuinely enjoying allowing herself to be pretty.

Somehow his business kept getting delayed—he'd now been on Cape Cod for nearly a week. It was the third night they had finished the day like this:

bringing the barbecue down onto the beach, talking, teasing, tormenting each other late into the night.

Last night, on the Fourth of July, instead of joining the crowds in town they had come here, to the place he was beginning to think of as *their* beach.

And as the sky had lit up with the fireworks from town they had floated in calm waters beneath the exploding rockets, staring up at a dazzling sky, the symphony of fire reflecting in the water all around them. It had easily been the most magical experience of his life, more magical than the first big-league game, more magical than the first huge renovation and successful sale.

Ethan, a man who could afford many pleasures, was being constantly awakened to the joy in the simplest of things: a freshening breeze stirring beach grass and her hair, watching her play tag with the dog.

Ethan knew it was getting late and he should take her home, but he had the feeling he'd had every day since he had met her, of not wanting to let go.

Sunday and Monday her business had been closed, but after that he had talked her into playing hooky. Amanda had moved home with her parents and was still holding out against Charlie. Despite her own romantic disaster, Amanda was taking absolute delight in he and Samantha's deepening relationship, and had volunteered to look after Groom to Grow for a couple of days. It was good for his cousin. She obviously needed something to do other than think about Charlie, and she had given them the gift of allowing them to have these wonderful first days of July together.

Today had been the most perfect day he could remember in a long time. Samantha had taken him for his first sailing lesson this morning on her beautiful little boat, the *Hall Way*. He'd been in awe of her expertise and agility, but mostly in awe of the look on her face as the wind caught in the sails: joy, freedom, connection with this world she lived in.

They'd had a long lunch, driven down the coast, explored parts of the Cape Cod National Seashore. She had taken him to a beach after, where they had dug clams for their supper. The day had been playful, honest, intense.

Just like this woman he was with, that he was coming to know, even as he felt a thirst to know her better.

He kissed her hair, ran his fingers through it. "I love your hair," he whispered, but he heard a deeper whisper, and didn't speak it.

Her hand covered his where he touched her hair, and he marveled at this comfort they had in each other.

"My hair is what reminded me I was a girl all those years growing up with my brothers. It would have been so much easier to cut it, and I remember coming close so many times, but in a way, it was what I had left of my mom."

Her voice went very soft as she continued, and he

knew he was being given another gift, maybe more spectacular than all the others.

She was giving him her trust.

"I could remember Mom brushing my hair, our bedtime routine. She would sit behind me and brush my hair until it crackled around my head, and she would tell me what a beautiful girl I was and how glad she was that I was hers, and how glad she was we had each other in our household full of men."

He touched her cheek, and found a tear had strayed down it. And he felt an enormous sense of gratitude for this gift of Sam's trust. After all these days of playing, she was going to show him her more vulnerable side, and he felt honored by her moving effortlessly into the next step between them.

"What happened to your parents?" he asked softly, stroking her hair.

"This is a beautiful place," she said quietly, nodding toward the sea, "and a hard place, too. It's unforgiving out there. And the more time you spend on the sea, the greater your chances of making the one mistake that it won't forgive.

"They loved to sail. They never lost that, even with all the hectic activity of raising four kids, they always carved out time for each other. It was almost as if that time alone with each other was sacred to them. They were very experienced, and they knew these waters, but a sudden storm blew in."

"I'm so sorry, Samantha."

"Thank you. Sometimes, now, all these years later, I feel moments of gratitude that they went together, because I really cannot imagine one of them being able to survive without the other, or one having to watch the other getting sick and dying a slow, painful death."

He realized, then, that Sam had seen real love, deep and abiding, and that was a part of who she really was as much as anything else. He had known her only a short, short while. How was it possible that he was wondering, already, if he could be worthy of that?

But he had known Bethany for eight months before he had popped the question. Time had not made him any more certain of what he was doing. He had confessed his doubt to his father, who had suggested he test her. Quit playing ball. See how long it lasted then. She had failed that test with flying colors!

He had known this woman for a week and felt a deeper sense of connection, of certainty.

Maybe love, of all things, was what most resisted man's efforts to put it in a box, to tame it with time, to place rules and restrictions around it. Maybe it just happened, even when it was inconvenient, even when it made no sense, especially when you were least expecting it.

Love. He had not said those words to her. But that is what his mind had whispered to him when he had stroked her hair. Ethan was shocked that they came to him so easily when he thought of Samantha.

"Still, it couldn't have been easy for you." He slid his hand along the delicate line of her shoulder, let it rest on her upper arm. Such a small gesture. And yet it filled him with a sense of possessiveness, tenderness, warmth.

"No, being a little girl in a totally male household was not easy. Mitch was newly married when we first arrived on his doorstep, me, Jake and Bryce. His wife couldn't handle the sudden death of the honeymoon. She left after a month."

Ethan remembered Sam's deeply cynical expression at the wedding and understood it.

Slowly she told him all of it. The trying to kill her own longing for things feminine because her brothers teased her so much about attempts to dress up, to look pretty, to put on makeup. She was embarrassed instead of overjoyed when she needed her first bra. Her brothers approved of toughness and disapproved of "sissy" things, and since that was her only safe harbor in the world, she became what they wanted her to be.

"I'm sorry," she said finally. "I shouldn't be telling you all of this."

"Why not? It seems to me maybe you've needed someone to tell for a very long time."

"I'm not condemning my brothers," she said hastily.

"I know that. I could see at the wedding their love

for you was very genuine. They just didn't know what you needed. Or not all of what you needed."

"Okay, I've spilled," she said, taking refuge in what he was coming to recognize as her sassy defense, what her brother had told him was tough-as-nails, and wasn't. Not even close. "Your turn."

And so he told her about growing up in a very wealthy family, and about how they hadn't approved when he had been drafted out of college to play major league ball.

"I had the college sweetheart. She was just what my big ego needed. I could do no wrong when I was a college star, and then when I was drafted to the Sox she went into love overdrive. Naturally I was swept off my feet, bought her the biggest diamond you can imagine and asked her to marry me.

"But you know, something in me thought something wasn't right. It was as if we were both playing roles instead of being real. Even though I didn't always get along with my father, especially back then, I went and talked to him. He suggested I tell her I was going to quit baseball and see what happened.

"She jumped ship as quickly as your sister-in-law, and it left me pretty disillusioned. I didn't want to lead a life anymore where people liked me because of what I did or what I had. So, I really did quit baseball and I signed off on the family fortune, too, which wasn't exactly what my dad had been expecting. I set out to make it on my own.

"I had the baseball money, and I had something to prove. Pretty soon, I was finding my relationship with business so much less fickle than my relationship with people. I turned all my substantial competitive nature on that.

"And you know what? It was enough for me. Until now."

And then he turned his face to her and kissed her. And realized once you had tasted someone like her, nothing else was ever going to be enough again.

And he knew it was time for something else.

She had brought him into her world. Now it was time to bring her to his.

"Come to Boston with me," he said softly. "Just for a few days."

She hesitated, but she was full of yearning when she said, "My brothers would kill me. Or you. It hasn't exactly been an accident that all our activities have not taken place in St. John's Cove."

Now that she mentioned that he recalled, even this morning, that her expression had been furtive until they had gotten that sailboat safely out of the harbor.

"The truth is," he told her softly, "that I appreciate the fact your brothers are so protective of you."

"Only because you haven't seen them in action. Last time I was on a date, Mitch showed up, and ever-so-casually mentioned his shotgun collection."

Ethan laughed, but she didn't see the humor. "I'll speak to your brothers," he reassured her. "If you come, it will all be aboveboard. I'll get you a hotel room."

"No," she said softly. "I guess it's time for me to speak to my brothers myself."

But all he heard was that she was coming, and he felt his heart soar upward like the kites they had flown the first day they had been together.

When Samantha got in that night, Amanda was just leaving the store, though it was very late.

"How are things between you and Charlie?" she asked hopefully.

Amanda shrugged, which Samantha took to mean an unfortunate *No progress,* especially when Amanda launched into a detailed blow-by-blow on what had sold at the store, and who had been in that day, deliberately avoiding the topic of her marriage.

"Oh, and the real estate agent brought somebody through. They asked if they could see the apartment, and I didn't know what to do, so I let her take them through. Is that okay?"

In truth, Sam hated the idea of someone touring her personal space. The real estate agent was supposed to give her forty-eight hours notice before showing it. But it was done, and really, there was probably no sense putting obstacles in the way of the sale.

She could *feel* change on the wind, ever since Amanda's wedding she could feel it. Only she didn't feel quite as frightened of it as she had a few short days ago.

In fact, she was aware her stomach didn't knot up at the news somebody had looked at the building, for the first time since it had been put up for sale.

"Amanda, Ethan asked me to spend a few days in Boston with him."

Amanda's delight was as short-lived as her own had been. "Don't tell your brothers," she said with a shudder. "Mitch will kill him."

"Thanks," Sam said dryly. And as tempting as it was not to tell Mitch, she had never lived her life like that and she wasn't starting now.

She picked up the phone. Despite her attempt at bravery, reminding herself that she was the one who made the first plunge into the ocean every year, Sam felt her stomach turn sideways when he answered.

"Mitch, I have to talk to you."

"Talk away, little sister."

But her stomach swooped again, making what she had felt about people looking at the building feel like a small upset.

"In person would be better."

"Is everything okay?" he asked, his voice rough with concern.

"Yes. I'll come over for coffee in the morning. See you then." Her hand was shaking when she hung up the phone.

And she still felt like she was shaking when he opened the door in the morning, pulled her into a crushing bear hug. Then he set her back at arm's length and frowned.

"You're all dressed up. Are you wearing makeup? What's going on? Are you going on a job interview? Did your building sell? I heard there were people looking at it."

That was a small town for you. It was only by the grace of God he hadn't heard about her taking Ethan sailing.

"Mitch, you can wear makeup for things other than going on a job interview!"

"It's a little early in the day for a wedding." And then his scowl deepened. "Uh-oh. A man."

She shoved by him and went into his messy kitchen, back to a typical bachelor pad now that she no longer lived there. She kept her back to him and poured a cup of coffee.

She took a sip, took a deep breath and turned back to him. "I'm nearly twenty-five years old, Mitch. Would a man be such a bad thing?"

"You're not going out with any guy I haven't vetted first, little girl!" His face was like thunder. He was unconsciously flexing and unflexing his huge arm muscle.

"Mitch," she said, "I'm not a little girl anymore."

And just by saying those words, she felt the power and the truth in them and suddenly she felt courageous and not afraid. It allowed her to see the fear in his protectiveness, and she felt tender for him, even though she knew it was time for her to move out of the shadow of his protection.

"I've met a really nice guy," she said, "and I'm going to go to Boston with him for a few days."

"Over my dead body!" he thundered.

"Mitch," she said softly. "I'm lonely. I want what Mom and Dad had. It's time for all of us to move past the pain of them dying, of Karina leaving us when we needed her most. It's time to start living again."

"I don't want you to get hurt," he said, more quietly. "That's all."

"I know that, Mitch. But you know what? I feel alive, fully alive for the first time in a long, long time. I feel as if I'm coming into myself, becoming the person I was always meant to be. I want to feel this way, even if it means taking a chance. And I want you to know this is the last time I'm coming to you about my personal life. I don't need your permission to live it as I see fit. My life is mine, not yours."

"You're firing me as your brother," Mitch said, astounded.

"No. I'm firing you as my parent, and asking you to be my brother."

He was silent for a long time, and then he gave his head a mighty shake and opened his arms. "Come here, little girl. I knew when I saw you all dolled up for the wedding it was only going to be a matter of time. I just wasn't expecting it to be quite this fast."

And she went into his arms, and let him hold her, and then she pulled away.

"Are you going to tell me who the guy is?" he asked as she headed for the door, feeling lighter than air.

"No."

"Ah, hell, do you think I'm just a dumb lobster-man? You tell Ethan Ballard if he hurts you, I'm gonna break both his legs. He doesn't need them since he gave up baseball, anyway."

And then, just when she wondered if he had heard a word she said, he softened the threat by winking at her.

Boston was exhilarating. They took the ferry, that ran only from June until September, from Provincetown Harbor to Boston. Once there, Ethan put her up in a harbor view room at the Boston Harbor Hotel. Located at the super-posh Rowes Wharf, the exquisite five-star accommodations overlooked the magnificent waterfront.

Then they became tourists in his town. Sam had been to Boston many times before, but had never enjoyed it so much as seeing it through his eyes. They went to antique stores and quaint little bistros. They strolled in parks and explored galleries and museums.

They even went on the famous ride-the-duck tour, part sightseeing excursion, part carnival ride. Old World War II DUKW amphibious vehicles charged into waterways and lumbered down streets to some of Boston's favorite must-sees. The "conducktors" had wonderful names like Major Tom Foolery and Commander Swampscott. Each vehicle had a name—theirs was Beantown Betty—and Sam couldn't remember when she had last found an experience so fun and refreshing.

Then there were quieter activities: a sublime dining experience at No. 9 Park, and a romantic one at Mistral.

She took advantage of the wonderful shopping available in Boston, not to scout out items for Groom to Grow as she normally would have done, but to upgrade her wardrobe yet again. She was delighting in the kind of clothes that appealed to her, subtly sexy and feminine, and she was delighting in feeling free to buy whatever she liked, not once imagining Mitch or Jake or Bryce rolling their eyes at her choices.

But Sam did have a moment when she wondered if she was getting in over her head. Ethan brought her to his place for a quick drink and change of clothes before he took her out for dinner. He owned a Back Bay house. It had started as one of his renovation projects, he explained to her, but the old house and the gas-lit neighborhood, located on a reclaimed seabed, had won his heart.

The house was incredible, the exterior and neighborhood reminiscent of nineteenth-century London, the interior modern, masculine and sleek.

For a few minutes, alone while he changed, she

felt acutely their social differences: she was a lobsterman's daughter. But as soon as he came back in the room, and grinned that now familiar grin at her, she felt the difference evaporate. He was just Ethan, not a multimillion dollar businessman.

On her last night there, he sprung it on her that they were having dinner with his parents at their Beacon Hill residence.

"That's why I didn't tell you sooner," Ethan said when she started fretting about what to wear and how to act. "Don't worry. You're going to be fine. I've got your back."

It turned out he was right. Once she got past being intimidated by the enormous wealth of John Ballard and his heiress wife she found his parents were engaging and good-humored. She'd expected stuffy and found them the furthest thing from it. She was particularly taken with his father, who came across as crusty at first, but whose love and concern for his son reminded her so much of the love and concern of her brothers.

On the surface maybe it would be hard to imagine two worlds further apart, the world of merchant banking and the world of lobster fishing, but Sam could see the common denominator of all people.

Love of family. Wanting a place to belong. Wanting to be liked and respected for who you were and not what you had or did.

When she said good-night to the Ballards, Ethan's

father took her hands in both of his, looked her deep in the eye and smiled before kissing her on her cheek.

He dropped her hands and looked at his son. "I like her," he said loudly. "She's a keeper."

And that was the other thing you could count on family for: they were always around to embarrass you with their love!

That night, after Ethan had gone home, she hugged herself and looked out her hotel room over the sparkling lights reflecting in Boston Harbor. There was no doubt in her that she was falling in love, and she could easily see why it was called *falling*. It was exhilarating, like swan-diving off a high cliff, blasting downhill on a roller coaster, launching into the water in Beantown Betty.

Samantha felt as if she had *finally* become a privileged member of a secret club. The club that *knew* why so many songs and stories, paintings and poems were inspired by *this* feeling. Alive, on fire, joy-filled.

She said out loud, "My life is perfect. More perfect than I could have ever imagined it. Even in my wildest dreams."

And she really should have known better. Saying something like that, even thinking it, was like tossing down a challenge to the gods.

CHAPTER SEVEN

AT THE last minute, Ethan had business to deal with and couldn't drive her home. He asked her to stay an extra few days, but Sam said no. She knew people had to continue functioning, difficult as that was when you were floating, when your life had become a love song, when you couldn't stop thinking of that other person's eyes. And mouth. The curve of his smile. The hard line of his muscled arm. The sound of his voice, like a gentle touch on the hairs on the back of your neck.

Still this was the longest she had ever been away from St. John's Cove and her business.

Not to mention her brothers and her friends. How were Amanda and Charlie doing? She suddenly felt guilty that she had escaped so completely that she hadn't even thought to call Amanda, that she had not once looked for stock for her store.

She wanted to take the bus back, but Ethan didn't like it, and insisted on renting her a car. After a drive home that seemed so boring *alone,* she turned in the car at St. John's Cove, and was given a ride home by Matthew Bellinger, the town's oldest bachelor. He told her, shyly, that he was taking Mable Saunders for tea the following day.

Love is in the air, Sam thought happily.

Ethan had insisted she call as soon as she got home so he knew she'd arrived safely, and Sam was so intent on that—and on hearing his voice again, how could she already miss him so completely—that at first she walked right by the sign that swung in front of her store, eager to share her happiness with Amanda who was just closing up inside.

But the bright red sticker grabbed her peripheral vision and she backtracked and stared with disbelief.

The happiness escaped from her with a nearly audible hiss, like air from a pricked balloon.

Sold.

How could that be? How could her life have changed so completely when she had just glanced away for a moment? But isn't that what happened when you let go of control? It was taken from you.

A boat due that never came home. If she had only noticed they were overdue sooner, taken control...

A familiar stomachache, a sensation Sam had not felt for days, twisted in her gut. She approached the door of Groom to Grow, the lightness gone from her step, feeling like a prisoner going to the gallows.

She opened the door and looked around at her

beautiful space as if she was already saying goodbye. This was her business. More, it was *home*.

And she, of all people, knew how quickly you could lose that place called home.

"Oh, Sam, I'm so sorry," Amanda said when she went in the door. Sam knew she had not succeeded at hiding her stricken expression. "They just came by and put up the Sold sticker minutes ago! I was going to try to get the sign down before you got here so I could break it to you gently. Are you okay?"

Actually Sam felt like she was holding it together by a thread, but she smiled bravely and made her escape out the front door and up to her apartment. If she let Amanda hug her, she would break into a million pieces.

She called Ethan and was relieved when she got his voice mail. She left a quick message saying she was home safely and hung up.

She dialed the Realtor, who wouldn't give her any more information than she had given Amanda, even though they were second cousins by marriage.

"You're the *tenant,* Sam. I can't divulge the details of the deal to you. It's between the owner and the purchaser."

"What about my business? What about Groom to Grow?"

"The possession date is only thirty days away."

"Thirty days?" she breathed. "Isn't that awfully fast?"

"To the owner's delight," the Realtor said dryly. "You'll be contacted soon, Sam. Don't worry."

Don't worry. She had spent the last wonderful week not worrying. And look what had happened. Logically she knew *worrying* would not have changed anything, but she had an awful feeling.

As if she had let down her vigilance and her whole life was being shot to smithereens because of it. While she was gallivanting around Cape Cod and Boston, she should have really been scouting a new location for her store! She should have been planning for this contingency, instead of letting herself be swept away.

The phone rang. She hoped it was the Realtor showing proper loyalty to family members, but it wasn't.

It was Ethan. Why did she feel mad at him?

Because he had made her *believe* for a short time that life held only good things.

"How was your trip back?"

For some reason, Sam steeled herself against the way his voice made her feel: as if she just wanted to blurt out every fear she'd ever had, lay them on his broad shoulders, let him help her carry them. It scared her that she didn't want to be *brave* anymore.

"Uneventful," she said. She couldn't trust herself to tell him about the store without crying, and the last thing she wanted to feel right now was more vulnerable.

"Hey, guess who called me this afternoon?"

"Who?"

"The Finkles. They want to meet with us again. What do you think of that?"

She felt as if her heart was doing a free fall, as if it was shooting down that hill in a roller coaster, only it wasn't going to make the turn. It was going to fly right off the track.

She'd always known she wasn't good enough. She'd always known better than to trust life. She thought of the Sold sign swinging gently in front of her store. And of him inviting her to go the Finkles, her blowing the deal the first time.

He'd said he didn't care. But he'd warned her he was competitive. Had everything since then been geared to this moment? How easy it would be for a man like him, worldly and successful, to make a little bumpkin like her believe.

He hadn't ever said he'd given up on Annie's Retreat. He'd said he was backing off "for the time being."

She thought of his eyes and his lips, the way his hand felt in hers, the way she tingled when any part of him came in contact with any part of her.

She thought of his father saying, She's a keeper.

No one could have gone to such lengths to keep a pretense going. No one. But even knowing that, knowing she was being unreasonable, suddenly she could not see any way they could have a happy ending.

This would end in heartbreak, one way or another.

A boat pulling away from a dock and never coming back. She could not survive it again. She had pretended, ever since it had happened, that she was strong. Tough as nails. Brave.

But she wasn't. The truth was she wasn't even brave enough to keep a dog; they passed through her life on the way to somewhere else, because she was afraid to keep them. Afraid to love totally.

And suddenly she didn't want anyone to know how afraid she was of change, good change or bad change, least of all not him. She did not want to be made weak and needy by love, she did not want to be powerless before it.

So, she thought, I will make him despise me.

"You planned it all, didn't you?" she demanded. "From the very beginning, this is what you wanted. For me to go back to the Finkles with you, and be convincing this time. Woman in love."

"What are you talking about?" he asked, genuinely baffled. And then, softly, "Are you a woman in love?"

"No!" Yes. "Would it have made you happy if I was? We could go back out to Annie's Retreat and get what you missed out on the first time. Of course, buying my store, the bride price, was putting the cart before the horse, but why not? You're used to getting what you want, aren't you?"

Stop it, she told herself, but she couldn't. This was safer, this was easier. She had kept her life as unchangeable as she could since her parents had died. She lived in the same place. She saw the same people. She had not even allowed herself to grow up. She was not ready for the kind of change Ethan Ballard represented.

"Buying your store?"

"Don't play the innocent with me! You're just like my brothers! You had to look after me. You couldn't believe I could make it on my own! You could get Annie's Retreat and bail me out at the same time!

"Get this straight, Ethan Ballard. I don't need your help and I don't need you!"

His long silence told her she was succeeding at driving him away, at keeping her world narrow and safe.

"How can you believe such a thing of me?" he asked quietly.

"You're the one who thought you could buy a bride," she reminded him, something in her voice so cold. So cold she was shivering, but he didn't have to know that, and he couldn't see her.

She could hear the thinly veiled fury in his voice when he said, "If that's how you feel, Samantha, goodbye."

She saw Amanda had come up the stairs behind her, not wanting her to be alone. She was staring at her wide-eyed as she set down the phone. A picture of composure, Sam plucked Waldo out from under Amanda's arm, tilted her chin and

went to her room, shut the door with a quiet click
behind her.

Still lugging Waldo she went over to the stereo in
her room and turned it on. Loud. A love song, naturally. And only then did she allow herself to cry at
what she had just done.

And over all the ridiculous things, because he
had always called her Samantha and never Sam and
she was going to miss the way he *saw* her so badly
it felt as if she might die.

She hugged the dog she was not keeping to her,
let him lick away her tears and thought, Tomorrow
I will find Waldo a new place to go, too.

Ethan hung up his phone, and stared at it with disbelief. He was aware he was shaking with fury, and
glad he was not anywhere near the delectable Miss
Hall at the moment. He might strangle her!

How could Samantha, after these intense days
together, not know who he was? How could she not
trust him? He thought he loved her, and she could
believe the absolute worst of him on so little evidence?

It was the most insulting thing that had ever
happened to him. He was astounded by the depth of
his hurt. He wanted to smash things. He wanted to
stand out on his balcony and yell obscenities at the
top of his lungs. He wanted to convince her she was
wrong, and in the next breath, he wanted to convince
her he was indifferent to her.

He did go stand on his balcony for a moment, and something in him quieted as the sea breeze touched his skin, reminded him of racing across the sand with her, kites behind them. He remembered bonfires, and laughter, digging for clams, swimming under a sky that was exploding.

And he remembered her face when she had looked at Annie's Retreat.

The wistfulness so naked in it, even though she had been trying to hide it.

And suddenly the truth came to him, as quiet as that breeze and just as comforting. She wanted to love him, and she was scared to death at the same time.

This wasn't about *him*. Love was asking him not to make it about him, to rise above his bruised ego and *see*.

And when he looked hard, what he saw was a little girl who had lost her parents at a young and impressionable age.

She had probably been scared to death to trust one single thing about life ever since then. What about her life would have made her believe, not just that good things happened, but that they stayed? Look at what had just happened to her business, the building sold out from under her, reinforcing her belief that nothing good could last, nothing good could stay.

No wonder she was afraid of what he had seen so clearly in her eyes.

She was falling in love with him.

That was going to be his job. To show her. That good things happened. And that they stayed. It was going to be his job to show her that she didn't have to sacrifice her independence to accept love, to not be lonely anymore.

He picked up the phone and called Annie and Artie Finkle. Artie was away but the next day Ethan sat with Annie in the little cottage Sam had loved. He told Annie the truth. All of it. That he had planned to trick them into thinking he was the ideal purchaser for their property. And that he had talked Samantha into going along with it by holding out a carrot he thought she couldn't resist, Groom to Grow. But she hadn't been able to compromise herself, and in that moment, when he had seen the uncompromising strength of her character, he had started to become what he had pretended to be, a man in love.

"Asking her to pretend to be my bride was my worst idea ever," he confessed. "Now she thinks," he said softly, "that I bought the store to win her over more completely, and that I just pretended to love her to get what I wanted from you. And it's not true."

"Of course it's not true," Annie said, and placed her wrinkled, age-spotted hand over his, comforting, *forgiving*. "You couldn't have bought her building. Artie and I did. I didn't realize Groom to Grow was Samantha's business, of course."

"You bought her building?" Ethan asked, stunned.

"I went there shortly after you and Sam had been here. I wanted a cute little hoodie for Josie like the one that Samantha had for her dog. When I saw the For Sale sign on the business, I arranged for Artie and I to see the apartment above it. I just fell in love with it—looking out over the park, over the store, all the wonderful original details giving it so much character.

"I just felt if we lived there we would still be so much a part of the community, not locked up in some gated community where you can't even hear children laugh! I'm going to open my shop there." She lowered her voice. "Artie needs something to do. Retirement is boring him to death. We saw some older gentlemen playing chess in the square the day we were there. I can't wait to be there, right in the heart of things."

"You bought it?" he asked again, and then had a flash of inspiration. "Can I buy it from you, then? I'll give it back to her, and this whole mess will be fixed."

"No," Annie said, smiling. "You can't and it won't. You see, son, you said that getting Samantha to pretend to be your fiancée was your worst idea ever, but in a way wasn't it the best thing that ever happened to you?"

He thought of those days with Sam, so filled with laughter and sunshine and discovery. It was true. His worst idea ever had given him the best days of his life.

"I call that a spirit-shot," Annie said softly, "when

our worst experiences, our mistakes, our lead, are spun into gold. When you get to be my age, you take comfort in knowing something greater than you is running the show."

Ethan thought of that: the string of coincidences that had led him to Sam, the impulses that had driven him, though he was the world's least impulsive man, the "mistake" that had made him deepen his relationship with her.

"I don't think what Samantha needs is her store back," Annie said. "I think maybe she's made that business fill all the spaces in her life that love is meant to fill. I think you are meant to marry that girl and give her the place we all long for."

"And what place is that?"

Annie looked around the coziness of her living room, her eyes brimming with love. "Home," she said softly. "Bring that girl home, young man."

CHAPTER EIGHT

ETHAN knocked on the door of the little fisherman's cottage. It seemed to him the place was badly in need of a feminine hand.

Mitch threw open the door, recognized him, and his whole face tightened. "You," he spat out. "Which leg do you want broken first?"

"Excuse me?"

"My little sister is a mess. Her eyes are nearly swollen shut from crying. She lost about ten pounds—that she can't afford to lose. She's letting Amanda run her business instead of going back to her husband where she belongs. Sam hasn't even been inside the door of Groom to Grow in four days. I may just seem like a dumb lobsterman to you, but I know what a broken heart looks like."

"You don't look like a dumb lobsterman to me," Ethan said evenly. "You look like a guy who would go to the ends of the earth to make sure his sister was happy. That's why I'm here."

Mitch looked at him suspiciously.

"I love her," Ethan said.

"Oh, sure, that's why she's bawling her eyes out as we speak."

"She's afraid to love me back, Mitch. You got any ideas where that would come from?"

Mitch took a sudden interest in his sock, which, in true bachelor style, had a large hole in it that his toe was protruding through.

"It was tough enough that she lost her folks," Ethan said quietly. "But then her brothers wouldn't get back in the game. So, she fell in love with her business, thinking that was safe. And now it looks like that isn't any safer than anything else she's ever loved in her life."

"It was safe for her to love me," Mitch said. "And Jake. And Bryce."

"That's why I'm here. I need your help. I need you to show her exactly how much you love her back."

"Why should I believe you know what's best for her? Why should I help you?" Mitch said, not quite convinced.

"Because, Mitch, I'm about to become your brother-in-law, and that means we're going to be putting up with each other and helping each other out for a long, long time."

Mitch's mouth fell open. He stared hard at Ethan. And then he gathered him up in a bear of a hug that nearly crushed his ribs.

* * *

The banging was at the door again.

"Amanda," Sam said over the soundtrack for *Shrek*, the movie she personally believed to be the most romantic of all time, "you have to talk to Charlie."

"That's not Charlie. He doesn't know I'm here watching a movie tonight."

"He drives around town looking for your car! It's heartbreaking. Give the guy a break." And more softly. "Please?"

"I'm talking to Charlie," Amanda said stubbornly, ignoring the knocking on the door, "when you talk to Ethan."

Well, that was a stalemate. Sam passed Amanda the bucket of Fudge Ripple and got up and answered the door.

It wasn't Charlie who stood there.

It was Mitch. And Jake. And Bryce. Despite Waldo growling ferociously at them, having decided to hate all things male, they were grinning like gorillas who had just hijacked the banana train. They were filthy. Covered in sawdust and sweat streaks, clothes dirty. She could tell they were exhausted and exhilarated at the same time.

"What are you doing here?" she demanded.

"Kidnapping," Bryce announced.

"Kidnapping?" Amanda said from the doorway. "How exciting!"

"You're going to be next if you don't smarten up

about Charlie," Bryce informed her darkly. "You're killing that guy."

"Mind your own business," Amanda told him snippily.

Samantha tried to take advantage of the interchange to slide toward the bathroom where she could lock the door, but Mitch caught her, picked her up, tossed her over his shoulder and headed down the steep stairs with her. The dog bit him.

He handed her easily to Jake and scooped up Waldo and placed him back inside the door. "I thought you were getting rid of that dog?"

"Nobody wants him," she said. It was true. She had interviewed about a dozen prospective owners for Waldo. Twice he'd even gone home with them. But he'd been back the next day, wagging his tail joyously when he saw her.

A moment later she was pinned between Bryce and Jake in the back seat of Mitch's station wagon.

"You stink," she told her brothers.

"That's what happens when you work around the clock," Bryce said.

"What's going on?" she asked him. "I was in the middle of a good movie. And a good bucket of ice cream."

"Oh, well," Bryce said. "You know where to find sympathy. In between—" he paused at Mitch's glare in the mirror, and came up with a version altered from the usual ribald ones the boys used "—sympathize and sympathetic in the dictionary."

Her brothers had mollycoddled her for about twenty-four hours after she had announced to them that she was never speaking to Ethan Ballard again. Her brothers' idea of mollycoddling was Mitch delivering fresh fish off the dock, Jake buying her a new fishing spool for her rod and Bryce cleaning the salt off her sailboat for her.

And then, obviously figuring that was enough tenderness, not wanting to turn her into a *wimp,* they'd stopped. Stopped calling, stopped dropping by, suddenly frantically busy. She'd assumed they were uncomfortable with the intensity of her emotion. Now she saw it differently.

Up to something. She really should have guessed sooner.

Suddenly, even though it was dark, she recognized the road they had turned onto. Or was it? The sign Annie's Retreat seemed to be missing.

"What are we doing here?" she whispered.

"We've been gettin' ready for a wedding," Jake announced.

Mitch turned around and reached over the seat, clubbed his brother on the ear—affectionately, but still making his point. "Shut up," he said. "Next thing you know, you'll be proposing for him."

"For who?" she demanded, but her brothers had

gone very silent. "Let me out," she said. "Let me out right now. I'll walk home!"

Mitch surprised her by complying; he slammed on the brakes. Jake bailed out and held the door for her.

And that's when she noticed the torches burning bright on both sides of the pathway.

"You just follow the light," Mitch said softly out his open window. "It will lead you home."

And then he backed the vehicle out of there, and left her standing alone. It seemed to her she had a choice to make.

She could stand there in the dark.

Or she could go toward the light.

And wasn't that a choice all people had to make, sooner or later? Wasn't that a choice she had made when she had spoken so cruelly to Ethan the night she had found out her store had sold?

She had decided to walk in darkness.

How often were people allowed to make that choice again?

Slowly, and then more and more rapidly, until she was running, she followed the path lit by the torches.

At the end of it was the cottage. A single light glowed within, the light of home, the light that every heart that had wandered until it was weary dreamed of seeing.

She was no longer making a choice. She was being guided by something bigger than herself as she put one foot in front of the other and walked to the door that Ethan held open for her.

He closed it behind her, and she looked at him, and seeing him so close made her realize she had missed him even more than she had thought, and she had thought she had missed him to the point of dying.

He looked as bad as her brothers, though at least he had showered. But the handsome plains of his face were whisker-roughened, and he looked utterly exhausted. And yet a light shone in his eyes that took her breath from her.

He said nothing. Just wrapped his arms around her, pulled her tight into himself, rested his chin on top of her head and sighed.

After a long time, she stepped back from him, drank in his face once more and then, finally, not liking that she was responsible for the torment she saw there, looked around.

The interior of the cottage had been completely gutted. All that remained were the original hardwood floors and the fireplace.

"You bought it," she whispered.

"I did. The bride price."

She could not believe the changes he had made. When she had first looked at this place, she had said it would be a crime to change it.

But then, she'd had a known allergy to change.

And looking at what he had done: at how the space had opened, how the light would pour into every corner in the daytime, at how it would *feel* in here, airy, bright, clean, she realized to not change would have been the crime.

And that was the crime she had been committing against herself. And against him.

She looked at him again and allowed herself to call him, in her mind, what he was to her. *Beloved.*

"I'm so sorry, Ethan. I'm so sorry for the accusations I made. It was never, ever about you. I've been terrified of change. I'm so mixed up…and so afraid."

She thought maybe it was the first time since her parents had died and she'd had brothers to live up to that she had admitted being afraid.

It didn't feel like a weakness to do it. It felt brave to let another person see, finally, who you really were.

"I know you're afraid," he said, "and I have some bad news for you. I didn't buy the store. Artie and Annie did. She wants to open her hand-painted-rug shop there. That's why they were suddenly so eager to sell, and why they called me back. I told them the truth about our first visit here."

Sam felt, looking at him, he was showing her what real bravery was. It was making a mistake, admitting it and then going on.

All this time, she had been so worried about losing Groom to Grow. How could it be possible that it felt so right that that lovely old couple had bought it?

Maybe it felt right because Sam had decided to be truly *brave* and that meant relying on your heart for your strength, not your house. Certainly not your business.

"It's time for you to come home, Sam. To me. And this place. So you don't have to be afraid anymore. I love you, Samantha Hall. I have loved you from the moment I saw you save that bouquet from the chocolate fountain when it was so apparent that was the last thing you wanted to do. I suppose I could live without you, but it seems like it would be a joyless existence, and I don't want it."

He went down on one knee, fished a box from his pocket, opened it.

Inside was a perfect, beautiful ring. The diamonds winked with captured light.

"I can't promise you a life where nothing bad ever happens," he said quietly. "I can't promise you a life with no more heartbreaks, much as I want to. But I can promise you days lived fully, that will fill us up with the strength to deal with life's blows when they come. I cannot imagine my life without you in it. I want you to marry me, for real this time."

"Oh, Ethan, I don't deserve—"

But he silenced her with a look. "It's kind of a yes or no thing."

"Yes," she said, and he slipped the ring onto her finger, picked her up and waltzed her around the enormous expanse of the room he had been working on, and even though the space was altered from what it had been when she first saw it, she *felt* it again.

The future shimmered in the room, danced with them. She could hear the laughter of friends, and the crying of babes, the squeals of children, the cheers of men watching baseball games, the quiet companionship of women.

She could feel the love of her parents, finally victorious, finally going on. Through her.

"Soon," he said breathlessly, not letting her go, burying his face in her neck, kissing it. "I have to marry you soon. Because I can't keep my hands off you much longer, and your brother Mitch will kill me if I don't do this the honorable way."

For a moment, she thought she might have to talk to Mitch again, remind him she was an adult woman. But then she realized she just had to surrender and let her brother love her the way he loved her. In time, he would see she was an adult, her actions speaking louder than her words, and then he would treat her like one.

"We're getting married the second we can get everything in order," she agreed, feeling the delicious, familiar heat of being with him.

"I figured the beach out front would be perfect for a wedding," Ethan said quietly. "And that this room would be big enough for a reception the way it is right now. Your brothers have been helping me. I didn't want to start putting it back together until I'd gone over the plan with you. I moved the nursery. And I wasn't sure how many bedrooms we needed for six kids. Do you put two, or three in each room?"

He was teasing her.

"Maybe we should just think about one to begin with."

"Maybe, though, this might be a good time to let you know my father was a twin."

They were teasing each other. And she had missed it the way a swimmer who went under missed breath.

"Don't forget to make room for Waldo," she said.

"I can't imagine it being home without him," he answered and she thought she would melt at the way he said *home* and at his sincerity.

He *wanted* Waldo. And so, she realized, did she. Waldo, and every other stray that came their way, and six kids. And nieces and nephews, and neighbors and friends and family.

"Welcome home, Samantha," he said softly.

"Welcome home, Ethan," she said and felt the truth of it as her heart opened completely to him.

Home was not her apartment above Groom to Grow, and it was not the home she had grown up in and shared with her brothers. It was not this house, either, even though she could sense the future here. She knew this place could be transient. It was just sticks and stones.

But there was a place that was not transient—it was the place their hearts found refuge and strength. And that place was with each other. *Together.* That was home. Nothing could put it asunder. Nothing. Not even death. Once it had been, that place existed forever.

That place was a universal place that all of the human family longed for and recognized when they found it. Sometimes it was called Love, and she called it that now, touching his face with wondrous fingers, and with welcome.

She chose what she saw as his dark eyes drank her in, as his lips tenderly caressed her fingertips.

Her heart, like a sailor who had been lost at sea, raced toward him, toward the Light of Home.

BEST MAN SAYS
I DO

BY

SHIRLEY JUMP

Dear Reader

It was a pleasure working with Cara Colter again on this book! We had such fun when we worked together on the *In a Fairy Tale World* continuity a few years ago, and when I found out I'd be paired with Cara for this project I just knew it would be a blast!

Readers often ask me about how the collaboration process works. I've been fortunate to work with generous and smart authors who have brought great ideas to the table. With Cara and I, one of us said 'beach', the other said 'Cape Cod', and before we knew it the town of St John's Cove was born.

Throughout the writing process we each would contact the other with questions, or to share details about our characters. We collaborated on the setting, the story behind the Group of Six, and a few of the secondary characters, so that readers would see continuity from one book to the next and feel as if they had dived right into St John's Cove when they picked up the second story.

The project wasn't without its challenges—any time you work with someone a part of the autonomy of writing is given up, and I moved house in the middle of this and had a couple of other life upheavals. But, because Cara and I knew each other so well from the previous continuity, those challenges were barely blips along the way.

I hope you enjoy the *Just Married!* duet—this two-book adventure in St John's Cove. There are some towns I create that I really wish were real, just so I could vacation there—and this is one of them!

Happy reading

Shirley

To my own group of six back home
Some best friends stay that way forever
No matter how many miles are between us

CHAPTER ONE

VIVIAN REILLY had made a career out of making an entrance.

Or at least, that's what some would say in St. John's Cove. She'd earned that reputation back in high school, and never quite lived it down.

So when she skidded in late to Samantha and Ethan Ballard's wedding reception, just as every guest was raising a glass to toast the new couple, there was no shortage of raised eyebrows and judgmental whispers. She could have explained her tardiness, but didn't.

She'd already been found guilty and sentenced to a lifetime of wagging tongues years ago.

So instead she smoothed her dress—dark blue, form-fitting and cut just above the knee—kicked off the heels she hated and sashayed barefoot across the sandy beach at Annie's Retreat as if she owned the place. She didn't, but she'd hung out on these beaches often enough as a kid to know every square inch. Amanda Weston, one of Vivian's oldest friends, waved to her from a small table set up in a cozy grouping down by the water's edge. Vivian waved back and started toward the friendly face.

She stopped midstep when she heard a familiar voice.

"To Samantha and Ethan, may your every dream come true, and may you have a lifetime of happiness."

Vivian pivoted back toward the group gathered on the steps of the cottage as everyone raised their glasses in a toast. Samantha, Ethan—

And Colton St. John.

Make that Mayor Colton St. John, and also, apparently, Ethan's best man. Colton managed to look both relaxed and sexy in a white shirt, open at the collar, and a black suit jacket. He tossed the newlyweds a grin, then sent his gaze over the gathered guests.

Stopping when he reached Vivian.

The whispers began to gain in volume. A group of people standing to her right said something about the mayor and Vivian and an incident back in high school. Self-consciousness dropped over Vivian like a twenty-pound coat. She swallowed hard.

They would not get to her. They never had, and they wouldn't now.

Colton St. John stepped off the porch and crossed the beach, a friendly, lopsided grin on his face.

He headed straight for the woman who had brought more trouble into his life than a hornet's nest in a closet. If she was smart, she would keep right on going toward Amanda, but instead she found herself reaching up to smooth her hair.

"You're late," he said, the grin widening. "Trying to upstage me?"

"No, just… I got tied up with something. Lost track of time."

"Or were you avoiding another wedding like the plague?"

"Of course not." Liar.

On the porch, Samantha and Ethan exchanged a long, tender kiss. The crowd applauded. Vivian joined in, but her hands didn't seem to clap as loud as everyone else's.

"Does this mean you're thinking of crossing over to the dark side and considering a trip down the aisle yourself?" Colton said.

"Heck, no. This—" she waved a hand around the outdoor space "—is the closest I like to get to a wedding. I wouldn't even be *here,* if Sam hadn't asked me to stay in town for her wedding, after I made the ultimate sacrifice and put on a bridesmaid dress for Amanda." She laughed, finally finding her footing in the easy banter. This was where she felt most comfortable with Colton, how she could maintain her distance with him. Laughter could be a very convenient wall. "I'd sooner be hog-tied and dragged through the mud than married."

He smirked. "Then consider me your cowboy."

A surge of something Vivian refused to call desire roared through her at that image. She'd simply been reading way too many romance novels, that was all.

Colton leaned forward, and brushed at her hair. Then he paused, his blue eyes meeting hers. "You have…sprinkles in your hair. Like…ice cream sprinkles."

Vivian inhaled sharply, and stood still. Very, very still. A pink sprinkle tumbled to the ground before her. Then another. Edible confetti littering the beach between her and Colton.

She'd seen Colton a dozen times over the last few weeks, since she had been back in town. He, Samantha, Bryce, Amanda, Charlie and she had been good friends forever. They'd grown up in the same neighborhood and banded together, eventually dubbing themselves the Group of Six.

Friends. That was how she had kept things with Colton for a long time. And how she had left them when she'd roared out of this town five years ago. She'd thought she could keep it that way, even as she ran into him again and again. And all these weeks, she'd done a pretty good job of convincing herself she had nothing but friendly feelings toward him.

Until he'd touched her.

Now an earthquake had rattled the foundation of everything she thought she'd known.

She let out a little laugh. The sound shook at the end. "I got hungry before I came here. Made a quick stop for a bite to eat. And while I was there things got…messy."

That was sort of the truth. She had stopped at an ice cream parlor. She had gotten messy. But only because she'd been pitching in, not dining in. Still, she wasn't about to share that particular detail with Colton. Or anyone.

He shook his head, chuckling. "Only you would do that. Viv, aren't you a little old for a food fight?"

She tossed him a grin. "Never too old for some fun, right, Colton?"

"I bet you have that motto tattooed on your ankle."

"Not on my ankle," she teased, showing him the bare skin of her leg.

Across the room, Amanda and Charlie Weston started arguing. Neither Vivian nor Colton could hear the words, but the facial gestures and tense postures said plenty about how the fight would end up. Sure enough, a moment later, Charlie stormed out of the reception, and Amanda went in the opposite direction, tears streaming down her face. Samantha followed along with Amanda, providing a comforting hug. The DJ announced dessert inside, as if reading the need for a distraction.

"You'd never know they just got married a few weeks ago," Colton said as he and Vivian headed inside Annie's Retreat along with the other guests. The cottage had been cleared to make room for more tables and a small temporary dance floor.

"I hope Amanda and Charlie work it out. They deserve a happy ending." Vivian sighed.

The melancholy note in her voice surprised Colton because it was so out of character for Vivian. He snuck a glance at her.

In his mind, he'd stamped Vivian with one label, and one label only: FRIEND. And for good reason, too.

Except for one crazy summer when he'd been twenty-three, she just over twenty-one, and he'd thought otherwise. Then Vivian had set him straight, and reminded him the two of them were all wrong for each other, and better off staying friends.

It was a lesson he'd never forgotten.

But something about the passage of time, about the years Vivian had spent in California, had changed those six letters. Made him reconsider everything he thought he knew about Vivian.

And turned her from FRIEND to WOW.

Okay, so that was only three letters, not six, but his brain kind of sputtered to a stop whenever he looked at her. The gangly teenager he'd hung out with had turned into a tall, leggy redhead with a cascade of curls and wide emerald-green eyes that both teased and captivated him. The woman she'd become had a powerful draw, ten times stronger than when she'd been a teenager. Even hotter than when she'd been in her early twenties. Like a fine wine, Vivian Reilly definitely aged well.

Yet, she still had that air of trouble about her, the same one that spelled all wrong for him.

Now, though, there was also something more, something he couldn't name.

Something almost…

Heartbroken.

Yeah, that was the word. That's what he'd seen in her eyes when she'd watched the bridal couple, when she'd seen Amanda and Charlie fighting. Only, thinking that about Viv was crazy. Of all his friends, Vivian Reilly would be the least likely to leave her heart vulnerable. She had always been the good-time girl, the partier. The one who could get him into trouble faster than he could spell the word.

Yet another reason to steer clear of her. The last thing the mayor of St. John's Cove needed in his life was trouble. Especially at this stage of his career, when he stood at a pivotal crossroads.

Except, he'd seen these flashes of another side of her, and that had his curiosity piqued. Had she changed, or was she the same Vivian he remembered?

"You seem different, Viv," Colton said. The July heat barely abated inside the building, despite several fans. Colton lifted the edge of his collar, as a bit of relief against the early July heat, grateful Ethan had opted to have his ushers wear open shirts, with no ties. Colton would rather be in jeans and a T-shirt than a tux—bow tie or no bow tie—any day. "More…subdued."

"Me? Subdued?" She let out a throaty laugh. "I don't think so."

"Hey, we all have to grow up sometime. Even—" Colton pretended to let out a shudder "—settle down. But not you, right? You've always been the queen of avoiding the noose of conformity."

"Yeah, that's me." Vivian was quiet for a moment, watching the guests on the temporary dance floor. She nudged him. "You want to get out of here?"

"I'm the best man. I'm supposed to stay, Viv."

"Says who?" She leaned forward and yanked the pin out of the boutonniere on his lapel. He inhaled, catching the deep jasmine scent of her perfume. Heady, strong, like her. "Weddings are the height of boring. You stood on the altar, said your toast. Your job here is done."

A second later, she flung the single white rose toward the nearest table. An elderly woman let out a squeal when the floral Frisbee narrowly winged her. "Let's do something…wild," Vivian said, walking her fingers up his lapel.

Sending a wild surge through his veins.

He shouldn't.

He was the *mayor*. *Wild* wasn't in the job description.

"Viv—"

"Come on, Colton. For old times' sake."

He remembered those old times. Remembered them very well. They were the whole reason people had whispered when Vivian walked in late. Why people glanced between himself and Vivian from time to time, as if they expected the two to run off and toilet paper someone's front yard at any second.

He glanced across the deep green expanse of lawn. His father may have died three years ago, but the shadow of his presence remained, like storm clouds on a summer day.

Maintain the St. John image, Edward would have said. *Behave with decorum. You are a representative of this town. You are, after all, and above all, a* St. John. *And this is St. John's Cove. Don't ever forget that.*

But there was a way to have both, Colton was sure. To insert a little of what he had missed so much. Being around Vivian and the Group of Six so much in the last few weeks had reminded him how much he missed, not just such good friends, but being surrounded by people who understood him. People who knew the real Colton St. John, not *Mayor* St. John, but the regular person he used to be, back before he'd gone to law school, long before he'd launched his political career. It was…refreshing to be around his friends. To feel like he could be himself.

"What exactly are you proposing, Vivian?" he asked, a grin curving up his face. "Because if I remember right, our old times got us into plenty of scrapes. Now I'm the mayor, and I'm supposed to be a good boy, you know."

Vivian grabbed his arm, her green eyes shining with a dare. A fire roared to life in Colton's gut, a fire he had learned a long time ago to tamp down, to ignore, especially when it came to Viv and her ideas.

But damned if he could quite remember why right now.

"Why don't you take a vacation from being a good boy, Colton St. John, and remind me what I left behind when I ditched this town five years ago."

Her voice was husky, low, and filled with the kind of temptation Colton knew led to only one thing—

Trouble.

The very thing he would do well to stay away from. Because if he didn't, he'd pay a price he knew damned well he couldn't afford.

Ah, but how sweet would it be to go back to those days? The days of the Six, the days when he didn't sweat the consequences?

The days when he'd considered Vivian Reilly as so much more than a friend? The days when he hadn't been a St. John, hadn't been mayor, but instead just a man, and she, just a woman?

Vivian smiled, crimson lips curving across a heart-shaped face. "You game?"

He glanced at the sparring husband and wife in the parking area, two good friends of his, but still two friends whose marital problems were a tangled web he didn't want to go near. He couldn't help them, even if he wanted to. It wasn't like he had any advice to offer about marriage. Behind him, the band launched into the "Electric Slide." Across the room, Samantha's elderly aunt grinned and waved at him, clearly hoping he'd join her on the parquet floor.

"Mayor St. John!" A burly man in a too-tight shirt came barreling through the crowd, waving at Colton. "Can I have a word?"

Bernie Kindle. A good man, but one who could talk the ears off a beagle. As much as Colton loved his job, the last thing he wanted to do right now was listen to Bernie's latest saga about his neighbors, or his ideas about traffic lights and stop signs.

Even the mayor liked a day off once in a while.

"Last chance," Vivian whispered.

And Colton took it, choosing for the first time in a long time, escape over duty.

CHAPTER TWO

IT DIDN'T take long for Colton to come to his senses. He might *entertain* the idea of escape, but that was about all he could afford to do—entertain it. He was happy with his career, and the last thing he wanted was to endanger that with a visit to the local jail.

"Viv, we can't be doing this kind of thing anymore."

She propped her fists on her hips and grinned at him. "And why not?"

"We're too old, for one. And it's illegal for another."

She dangled a bikini in front of him—the same one she'd whipped out of her voluminous tote bag a minute earlier—the bright pink material a teasing temptation to walk on the wild side. "That never stopped us before."

Before.

The night before high school graduation. Same time of year, same time of night. The Group of Six had partied on the beach, then Vivian had asked Colton to drive her home. On the way, they'd gotten into a game of Truth or Dare. And when Colton had opted for Dare, they'd ended up at this very same place—only that time they'd gone all in—

Into Ely Hardisty's in-ground pool.

They hadn't bothered with swimsuits. They'd simply jumped in, clothes and all. And jumped out almost as fast when Ely came charging out of his house with a 40-odd aimed at Colton's head.

Ely had installed a six-foot chain-link fence the following week, and a half dozen KEEP OUT signs, along with a number of posted reminders about the legal ramifications for trespassing. Now Vivian was proposing they scale the fence, take a dip in Ely's pool, and all before the next neighborhood patrol car swung by.

"Vivian, you don't understand. I'm the mayor now. I can't be doing stuff like this." He started to turn away.

She grabbed his arm. "Who's going to catch us? Or know? My dad said Ely went down to Florida to visit his sister. The lights are off—there are no signs of life inside the house." She pivoted back toward the pool, the dare still shining in her eyes, twice as tempting now. "No one's here."

"Except you. And me."

"Yeah," she breathed. "Except us."

"We could get into trouble."

"Trouble… Isn't that what we used to be good at?" She grinned. "Come on, Colton, live a little."

He took a step closer to Vivian, winnowing a space that was already too close, too tight. For the last three hours, while they'd been at the wedding, Vivian had tried not to be distracted by the sight of Colton St. John in an open-shirted tux, giving her just a hint of the chest below. Had tried to see him as the friend he'd always been, not as the man he had clearly become in the years she'd been away.

A very intriguing, very handsome man. Tall, lean, blue eyes, dark hair with a slight wave that called out to be touched. He had the angular good looks of every St. John before him, but with a mischievous edge, as if there'd been an extra gene in his DNA.

Didn't matter. She wasn't the type to date—or for that matter, settle down—with a St. John. Too many rules, too many expectations. Too many—

Everything.

Colton St. John came in a very nice package, yes, but a package with a whole lot of strings.

And if there was one thing Vivian didn't need, it was strings tying her down.

Then why was she here, involving herself with Colton, the one man she'd never been able to forget, no matter how many miles she'd put between them? She'd moved all the way across the country—with another man, no less—and still seen Colton's eyes when she went to sleep at night. Still heard Colton's voice in her dreams.

And also still heard the warnings about staying

far from the next St. John political star. He was on his trajectory, she on hers—and they were moving in two different directions.

"Vivian, thanks for the offer, but I should get going. I have an early meeting tomorrow and I need to get some sleep."

She laughed. "You're sounding like a suit-and-tie guy now."

"Well, that's part of being mayor. Though I wear a tie as rarely as possible." The grin she remembered lit up his face, telling her the old Colton was still in there, at least in some part. "*That* hasn't changed."

But a lot of other things had. She sensed a distance between them, a measure of discomfort, as if they no longer knew each other. They had been the best of friends—more, once—and had known each other better than anyone else in town.

Unbidden, Vivian's gaze traveled over Colton's steely frame. In the last few years, he'd gotten taller, leaner, and more—

Everything.

She'd noticed, certainly, over the few weeks they'd spent together off and on since Amanda and Charlie's wedding, but not closely. After all, this was the first chance she'd had to be alone with Colton for an extended period of time. They'd had moments, sure, when they'd found themselves getting a drink out of Samantha's kitchen at the same time or sitting beside each other at a karaoke bar. But this was different.

This time, she was completely alone with him… and his very, very nice partially exposed chest. All hard planes and well developed muscles. The kind that said, *Lean on me, I'm not going anywhere.*

She would have done just that. If she'd been the kind to lean on a man.

This Colton, this grown-up, sometimes-tie-wearing Colton, she didn't know. And even though she'd lost interest in the pool, she couldn't let go of the search for the Colton she used to know. He was in there, she was sure of it.

If it took getting him into a pair of swim trunks to find him, then that's what she'd do. Especially if that had the added bonus of getting him to bare his chest.

Vivian dragged her attention away from his pecs, and back to his face. A charge raced through her veins. What was she doing, staring at Colton like that? They were friends, as they should be.

Not to mention she needed a relationship right now like she needed an extra foot.

Her life was exactly the way she liked it. Unencumbered. It had taken some doing to get back to that state. No way was she going to go and tie herself down again.

No way.

Uh-huh. "Come on, Colton, aren't you hot?" she asked, feeling a very different heat rising in her body.

He stepped closer. She inhaled. In the moonlight, his eyes glittered, then seemed to darken. "Of course. It's July, Viv. It's always hot this time of year."

A smile curved up her lips, as if she knew he'd purposely circumvented the innuendo. "Then let's get cooled off."

Oh boy. Colton had ideas for doing just that—ideas that had nothing to do with the pool glinting in the moonlight a few feet away.

He needed to remember this was *Vivian,* the girl he'd known for as long as he could remember. She was his friend. Nothing more. She'd told him that in no uncertain terms.

Regardless of a momentary flicker of change in their relationship a few years ago, he'd be crazy to think they were anything other than friends. After all, she'd moved on—moved in with someone else, last he'd heard—and so had he. No reason to rehash past history.

How easy it would be to fall back into the same old world he'd lived in before. The one where he didn't worry what people thought of him, didn't worry about the consequences of his actions. He simply did what he wanted because he wanted to. But that was then, and this was now—

And now he was a different man.

"I'm not going to trespass in a constituent's pool, Vivian. Sorry." He shrugged off her arm and stepped away.

"What? You're leaving?"

"When you said let's go do something fun, Viv, I thought you meant karaoke or…" He threw up his hands, trying to think of another option. "Something."

"*This* was something."

"This is crazy. Career suicide."

She laughed. "Since when have you worried about your career?"

"I've changed, Vivian, since you left. I'm not the same person."

"I'll say. The Colton I remember never would have said no to something like this. He would have been the first one over the fence."

"That man…" Colton eyed the fence, the one installed all those years ago, and saw it not just as a mesh of wire and steel poles, but as a metaphor for what separated him from who he used to be and who he had become. "Is gone. And for the better. We all need to grow up sometime."

"Where's the fun in that?" She called out.

But Colton was already gone. Vivian was talking to herself.

CHAPTER THREE

VIVIAN drove away, after dropping Colton off at his car, and watched him in her rearview mirror, heading in the opposite direction. To the other side of the tracks, literally. Vivian stepped on the rental car's accelerator and the six-cylinder pulsed forward.

What had she been thinking?

She hadn't been, that was clear. Her hormones had been the ones in the driver's seat.

For a few minutes there, she'd almost…almost gotten involved with Colton again. When she'd arrived in town a few weeks ago, she hadn't intended to do much more than say, *Hello, how you doing* to him. Maybe ask a few benign questions about work, throw him a comment about the weather.

In short, maintain the status quo until she went back to L.A. She'd done a good job of doing that—until tonight.

Colton St. John represented everything she'd run from, everything she didn't want, everything that was all wrong for her. When people thought of St. John's Cove, they thought of the St. John men. Generations of them, who had first built the seaside town, and then run it. And now, Colton had become *mayor.*

After what he told her tonight, a mayor who was happy running this town. Happy with the limelight, the restrictive life, the demands on his time. Whereas Vivian…

Wasn't.

If that didn't spell mixing oil with water, nothing did.

The small car darted down the dark, silent streets of St. John's Cove and into the town square. At the center of the deserted park stood the massive bronze statue of the town's founder—Colton's great-grandfather. He had passed down the same devilish good looks to his descendants, but thankfully, Colton hadn't inherited the stuffy sternness the statue's visage held.

Along Main Street, the colorful awnings had been rolled back. She noted the newest shop on the block—an ice cream shop, and the only one without an awning. The gaslight-style streetlights cast a golden glow over the haunts of her teenage years—the Clam Digger, Artie's T-shirt Shop, Pixie's Penny Candies. Vivian knew the small town like the back of her hand. Didn't matter how many years or miles she put between herself and the Massachusetts coast, every time she came home, it was as if she'd never left.

That was the whole problem. Being here brought up too many memories. Too much unfinished business. Like the entire reason why she shouldn't date a "good boy" like Colton St. John—

And why someone like her should just stick to the heartbreakers. Men like that didn't come with lives full of expectations and obligations.

Vivian shook off the thoughts and pulled into her father's driveway, located far from the beach, on the outskirts of St. John's Cove. She parked the car, got out and headed into the small ranch-style house.

Stay away from Colton. Before you break his heart again.

Or worse, break your own.

"So, how was the wedding?"

Vivian started at the sound of her father's voice. She crossed to the living room, the only light coming from the television, the black-and-white movie playing on the big screen creating an almost strobe-like affect. "Typical," she said. "Romantic and fancy."

"Probably cost an arm and a leg, too." He chuckled. "I take it you left early? Ran for the hills?"

She dropped into the armchair across from Daniel Reilly. The well-worn fabric had once been bright crimson, dotted with white roses. Now it looked more like a trampled, muddy garden. "I stayed through the vows. Even made it to the first course."

"Someday, you'll make it past the cake. I even have hope you'll hold on for the last dance." On the screen, Humphrey Bogart's gravelly voice and casual stance maintained his manly distance from the love of his life.

Vivian snorted. "That'll be the day."

"Yeah, the day you get married."

She rolled her eyes. "Dad, you should know me better than that. If you wanted a daughter who was going to settle down, you should have had more than one kid."

Daniel took a sip of the beer on the TV tray beside him, feigning interest in the movie that he'd now muted. "I kinda like the one I got."

"And you're not such a bad father."

He gave her a grin. A moment passed, while Daniel fiddled with the remote, avoiding Vivian's gaze. "Have you gone to see your mother yet?"

"I'm only in town for a few more days, Dad." That was the plan, at least. Stay a couple days, do what she needed to do, then get back to her life on the West Coast.

"This is such a big town you can't drive two miles?" Daniel paused, and when he spoke again, his voice was nearly as muted as the television. "It'll do you good to say what you need to say."

Vivian rose, her gaze on the television, not meeting the questions in her father's eyes. Humphrey Bogart was walking out of the room, probably leaving a whole lot unsaid himself. "I can't, Dad. I just…can't. It's too hard."

"Closing the door on your past doesn't mean the mess doesn't exist."

"Maybe. But it also means I don't have to deal with it, either." Then she said good-night and left the room.

Colton's office was busier than Grand Central Station.

Before ten in the morning on Sunday, he had dealt with more than a dozen town concerns, from the cuts in next year's budget to the missing stop sign at the intersection of Walnut and Bayberry.

He was glad for the distraction of work. Last night with Vivian had raised more questions than answers, and it was only here, buried in a mountain of community challenges, that Colton found his center again.

Sort of.

He kept picking up his pen, and a pile of papers, and though he saw the words, the columns of numbers, in the back of his mind he kept seeing Vivian, too. Kept hearing her voice.

Remind me what I left behind... Trouble... Isn't that what we used to be good at?

A long time ago, maybe yes. For years, they'd been friends who'd broken nearly every rule there was in St. John's Cove, driving his father insane and setting off more than one argument in the St. John household. The more Edward dug in his heels about Vivian's presence in Colton's life, the more Colton rebelled and headed out the door.

For so long, Vivian had simply been the girl down the street, his best friend—and partner in crime. Then one day when he'd been home on a break from college, he'd started to see her with new eyes. His heart had started skipping a beat every time she walked into a room. That summer, they'd gone from being friends to lovers, and Colton had imagined a future that included Vivian.

It had turned out to be a three-month mistake. One he was over.

Or so he thought. Until Vivian had returned, looking even more desirable than she had five years before. Only one adjective described her now—

Incredible.

But she was also incredible trouble. He knew where getting involved with Vivian could lead— straight down Heartbreak Lane. And that was a road Colton had no intentions of heading down.

A knock sounded on his door. Bryce popped his head inside Colton's office. "Working on a weekend?"

Colton leaned back in his chair and stretched. "What's a weekend?"

Bryce chuckled and entered the room when Colton beckoned him to sit. "I don't remember you being such a workaholic when we were kids."

"I wasn't. I…grew into this." And he had. In the three years he had been mayor, Colton had grown to love the job. To look forward to each day more and more.

When his father had been alive, Colton had bucked the political career yoke like a young colt being fitted for a saddle. He'd fought Edward St. John every step of the way, telling his father he had no intentions of following in the family footsteps.

Bryce looked around the office, at the books, files and papers that filled the shelves. "Seems you have, and then some. I hear you're planning on running for governor."

Colton nodded. "I haven't filed yet, but yes, that's the plan."

"On and up the political ladder, huh?" Bryce sat in the dark brown leather chair across from Colton. "So, you enjoy this?"

"What, being mayor? Yeah, more than I thought I would."

Bryce arched a brow. "Really? I thought you had other plans, meaning any other than politics."

"I did. Until my father died, and then the townspeople asked me to take his place, just until the next election. Those few months I spent filling in…" Colton shrugged. "I guess it made me see this job in a new light. I can make a difference here, even if it's just a small town."

"Small town to some, the whole world to others," Bryce said. "People who have lived here all their lives, the decisions you make matter to them."

"That's part of what makes this job challenging as hell, but also rewarding. The streets don't get plowed fast enough, I've got people calling me to complain at six in the morning." He chuckled softly. "But secure a federal grant to build a new library, and everyone in town thinks I'm a hero."

Bryce grinned. "While your friends know the truth."

Colton echoed the smile. "Oh, yeah? And what's that?"

"That you, my friend, are a mere mortal." Bryce rose. "Even if you're one who can move books and buildings."

"How long do you think you'll be able to keep up this crazy arrangement?"

Vivian dipped into her bowl of triple chocolate ice cream, but didn't eat the frozen treat on her spoon. She paused a moment, to look around the bright yellow, pink and white room, the paint still so fresh it nearly gleamed. The shop had become exactly what she'd always dreamed—and more. For five years, she'd scrimped and saved, putting every one of her tips in a jar, then a bank account, building her nest egg until she had enough to open her own business. The Frozen Scoop was the first of many like it, she hoped. Her dream had finally become a reality, and she could only pray the waffle cones and banana splits turned a profit.

"Forever," Vivian responded, then wagged her spoon at Kelly Hurley. "And it's not so crazy, Kelly. Lots of business owners do exactly what I'm doing."

"What would be so bad about staying here and running this place yourself, Viv?" Kelly, who'd been Vivian's friend for years, leaned against the wall behind the front counter of the Frozen Scoop, the ice cream parlor Vivian had opened two weeks ago. Dark wash jeans and a light blue T-shirt hugged Kelly's curvy frame, and she'd swooped her chestnut hair into a loose ponytail. "What, are you afraid people might think the wild child is finally settling down? Even *you* are allowed to have a life, you know."

"I do have one."

"I meant one with something—and someone—to come home to."

Vivian's gaze went to Kelly's left hand, to the simple gold band adorning her ring finger. Of all the people Vivian had known, Kelly was the last one she would have expected to settle down and live the suburbia life. Yet here she was, wearing a wedding band, sporting a "My Kid is an Honor Student" sticker on her minivan and working at a small-town store.

For a second, a flash of envy roared in Vivian's gut, then she pushed it away. Regardless of how much of a sales job Kelly tried to give the benefits of "settling down," Vivian knew better. She'd considered making a stab at that "normal" life once before—

And had it backfire in her face like a twenty-year-old car in need of a tune-up.

"I can run this shop from California," Vivian said.

"You do the day-to-day, I do the behind-the-scenes. Easy as pie."

"I love working here, don't get me wrong. I think you're doing a great thing with the kids you hired." She lowered her voice and gestured toward the kitchen, where Rosanna Simmons and Jimmy Penner, the first two hires, were busy doing dishes and cleaning up from the lunch crowd. The two teens laughed quietly as they worked, a dramatic shift in the sullen attitudes they'd had a few weeks ago. Simply seeing them change their views on life, to see that a future existed for kids like them—

The reward outweighed any financial benefit Vivian could ever imagine.

"I've really seen a difference in those kids, just in the few weeks we've been open. Who knew ice cream could have such power?" Kelly grinned. "And I love working for you, but…"

"What?" Vivian prompted when Kelly didn't finish.

"When are you going to take a risk?"

"Are you kidding me? Risk is my middle name."

Kelly snorted. "Right. That's why you're running back to California the first chance you get. If you're going to buy a business, stay here and run it, don't drop off some money and rush out the door."

Vivian winced. That had pretty much been exactly how she'd opened the ice cream shop. She'd planned on being in town only long enough to choose the location, offer Kelly the job as manager, then hire the contractors who had turned the former antiques shop into a bright, cheery treat stop. After that, she would oversee the Frozen Scoop entirely by phone and e-mail.

Allowing her to stay far, far away from St. John's Cove. The best plan all around.

"This is an investment, Kelly, not a career."

Okay, so it wasn't much as investments went. One ice cream shop wasn't going to pour profits into her pockets.

Then what are you doing surrounded by chocolate mint and cherry cordial?

Kelly pushed off from the wall and crossed to Vivian. "This is all about that day in Mrs. Simmons's class, isn't it?"

"A little. Maybe." Vivian turned away before her friend reached her, and toyed with an extra spoon on the pink-and-black-speckled tabletop. Sophomore year of high school, she'd had an assignment to write an essay about her dreams for her future. For the first time in her life, Vivian Reilly wrote down the God's honest truth.

She wanted to own a little ice cream parlor. Marry the man of her dreams, live in a pretty white house with a fence and raise two children, a boy and a girl.

Writing the essay hadn't been the bad part. Being told half the grade was based on delivering it orally was. She would have refused—but her English grade was already on shaky ground, and she'd spent enough time in detention to last her a lifetime. So she'd read her essay to the class—

And heard the snickers almost from the first word. No one could believe Vivian Reilly, party girl, wanted anything so "cheesy." At the end of class, Colton had come up to her and said, "That was a joke, wasn't it, Viv? That whole thing about you wanting to settle down, spend your life doling out double scoops?"

Instead of telling him the truth, she'd just nodded and affected a cool sneer. "Of course. Who wants that? I was just trying to get a good grade."

That had been the end of that. The only one she'd confided in had been Kelly, because if she'd told any of the Group of Six that the essay had been true, word would have gotten back to Colton. Even back then, she'd been half infatuated with him, and she couldn't stand to hear him laugh at her dream. She could only pray he'd forgotten the whole incident since then.

"Okay," Vivian conceded. "So maybe for a split second, I dreamed of living a normal life. Open up a place like this, run it during the day, and..." Her voice trailed off.

"Go home to a husband and two kids every night," Kelly finished for her.

Vivian scowled and held up two slim pieces of paper to the bright sunlight streaming through the plate-glass windows. "You know what this place needs? An awning. I was thinking striped. White and…which color? Cotton Candy Pink or Light Lemon Yellow?"

"Viv, it's not a crime to want a regular life."

"Definitely the yellow." Vivian waged the color chip. "It seems more friendly. And it matches the sign better."

Kelly sighed, clearly sensing it was time to drop the subject. "The yellow for sure," she said. "It'll invite people in, whether the owner's here or not."

Colton had never seen a man look more miserable. "Here."

Charlie took the opened beer, and nodded his gratitude. "Thanks."

Colton settled in the second Adirondack chair, and propped his own drink on the small table to his right. Night had begun to fall, draping a soft blanket of deep purple over the manicured one-acre yard. Dozens of flowering plants and fancy shrubs lined the space, plants Colton couldn't name and didn't tend. He rarely had time anymore to enjoy the yard, and had finally hired a landscaper to take care of it.

He missed the simplicity of taking time to plant a tree, trim branches. He could see his future ahead of him—the same life his father had lived—filled with political events, endless days in the office and the inevitable campaigning, and knew that investment of time came with the reward of building the community he loved.

He might not be able to make a difference with the rhododendrons, but at least he would with the streets and businesses.

Charlie let out a long sigh. "I never thought marriage was supposed to be like this."

"It'll get better. You guys have been together for a long time," Colton said, returning to his friend's problems instead of his own. "Plus, we've all been friends forever. You'll work it out."

Charlie harrumphed.

"Did you ever think it might be hormones? You know, her being pregnant and all?"

"I did. And I said that to her when we argued about going to my mother's. At Sam and Ethan's wedding." Charlie glanced over at Colton. "That's when she threw her shoe at me."

"Oh." Colton took a sip of beer. *"Oh."*

"Yeah." Charlie took a longer gulp. "She's still mad at me for telling my mother she was pregnant when we got married. She thinks I married her because…" He let out a sigh.

"Because you had to."

Charlie nodded.

"Did you?"

"Hell, no. I love Mandy. She's just not listening to me when I tell her that." He glanced down at the beer. "Do me a favor, Colton. Don't get married. It's way overrated."

"Marriage is not in my plans, Charlie."

That empty feeling returned again, as if Colton was missing out on something. He poured himself into his job, and yes, found fulfillment there, but a part of him wondered—

Was that all there was?

Marrying a life of politics with a regular life, though…Colton couldn't see it happening. Not for him, not for his father, and not for his grandfather. Not a single St. John man had been happy in his marriage. Edward had picked the "right" woman, something he had lectured his son about over and over again, as if a wife were a registered pedigree puppy.

Colton had no intentions of making the same mistake. He'd already seen how that kind of preordained union worked out.

Better to stay single. Much better.

"Trouble is, I'm already married." Charlie twirled the bottle between his palms. "And I love her. Love her more than anything."

"Then go talk to her."

Charlie glanced at Colton. "Come on, Colton. You know Mandy. She's stubborn. I've been talking for the last month, and it's gotten me exactly nowhere. We're right back where we started." Charlie rose, leaving the beer bottle on the small table. "Which is circling around the big *D* word."

He let out a curse and then he was gone, leaving behind a heavy air of sadness.

Colton sat there for a while, wishing he could do something to help two of his best friends work out their problems. But really, what could he do? Go talk to Amanda? And what would he say?

Best to stay out of it.

Charlie's sorrow gnawed at Colton. Enough that he abandoned his half-finished drink, and headed out of his house and down the street toward the one person who knew both Charlie and Amanda as well as he did.

Vivian.

CHAPTER FOUR

HER father was grinning—never a good sign.

Vivian put down her pencil, and pushed aside the legal pad she'd been jotting notes on, all plans for the Frozen Scoop. Business had been good at the shop ever since the doors had opened, and now Vivian was running the numbers to see about hiring more help for August and September. There were so many teenagers—too many—that she wanted to give a helping hand to, provide with a new direction, a vision of a future. The Frozen Scoop might not be able to employ them all, but she'd do what she could.

"What?" she said to her father.

"Someone's here to see you." He practically sang the words.

She eyed him with suspicion. "What has you so chipper? Have you been sneaking pie again? You know what the doctor said about watching your cholesterol."

"I'm dessert free." Daniel held up his hands as

evidence. "Now come on out and say hello. It's not like we have company marching through this door every five minutes, you know."

Vivian shook her head, then rose and headed into the living room, figuring Kelly had stopped by to try once again to persuade her to stay in town and operate the ice cream parlor herself. "I'm not going to—"

She stopped talking.

Colton stood in the living room, tall and impossibly handsome. Just by his sheer presence, he had a way of tempting her to stay awhile, to linger in the one place she'd never wanted to hang around. There was just something about the way he stood, the deep comfort in his blue eyes, that called to her. And that was dangerous.

She needed to head back to L.A. Immediately. Staying in St. John's Cove would have her considering crazy thoughts—like getting involved with Colton.

"Hey, Viv."

"What are you doing here?"

"Nice to see you, too." He grinned.

"I didn't mean that, I meant—" She glanced over her shoulder. "Dad, I'm not seventeen anymore."

Daniel harrumphed. "At seventeen, you were climbing out your bedroom window and hopping on the back of a motorcycle at two in the morning. This is the most traditional date you've ever had."

"This is not a date. Colton's a—"

"Friend," Colton finished for her.

Her gaze met Colton's and something Vivian refused to call disappointment sank in her gut. "Exactly. A friend."

The way she wanted things to stay.

Uh-huh. Then why did her heart skip a beat when a grin curved across Colton's face?

"You've been a hell of a mayor, Colton. I've really noticed a difference in this town since you took over." Daniel leaned in conspiratorially. "If you don't mind my saying so, you do a better job than your father. You relate to people. Talk to 'em. And even better, listen to their problems. Then, surprise, surprise for a politician, you *solve* 'em."

Colton chuckled. "Thank you, sir."

"Yep, this town is better for having you." Daniel glanced at his daughter, then back at Colton.

She could feel her father staring at the two of them, as rapt as a preschooler in front of a full cookie jar. She could stay here, and let this soap opera unfold with a patriarchal audience, or take the conversation somewhere private.

"I was just about to go out for a bite to eat," she said to Colton. "You want to come with me?"

"We just had dinner," Daniel cut in. "You and Colton should stay here. Have a soda, some barbecue chips. A snack, ya know?"

"Thanks, Dad, but I was thinking more like—"

"Wings at O'Reilly's?" Colton said.

Their old hangout. The place they'd both loved, for its anonymity and easy style. "You read my mind."

And then she was gone, before her father threw some potato skins under the broiler. And started quizzing Colton about his intentions. If there was one person in town who *did* want to see Colton and Vivian together, it was her father.

Vivian climbed into the passenger's seat of Colton's Mercedes. The luxury vehicle wrapped her in a cocoon of quiet and lush, comfortable leather. "Let me guess. You came by to check up on me? Make sure I wasn't expanding my crime wave to something bigger, beyond sneaking into the neighbor's pool?"

"Like grand theft auto?" he finished before she could.

Vivian laughed. "That was a fun night, wasn't it?"

"One of the best memories of my teen years."

She noticed the distance he added at the end—teen years. Another signal Colton had put those moments behind him. He had moved on, past whatever he and Vivian might have had in common.

Still, some masochistic part of her kept searching for the thread that used to extend between them. "Well, you know who to call, next time you want help putting the principal's car on the roof of the high school."

"Not to mention helping to steal that crane—"

"We were *borrowing* it, Colton. Get your terms right." She laughed.

"Okay, borrowing. Too bad the St. John's Cove cops didn't agree."

"Until your father talked the company into dropping all charges," Vivian pointed out. "Thank goodness, because we would have been in *so* much trouble if they didn't. We were stupid teenagers back then, weren't we?"

That was the Colton she remembered, not this more formal, all-business Colton who had clearly become *mayor.* Who had stepped into the very shoes he had fought so hard not to wear.

Why? What had changed?

"That stunt cost me a year's allowance and two months of privileges." He chuckled softly. "And it was worth every second of the home confinement."

"And I spent a week in the principal's office, doing all my class work 'under supervision.'" Vivian laughed. "Of course, I probably needed a lot of that in those days."

"You weren't the only one," Colton said. "We got into a lot of trouble back then. Fun trouble, but trouble all the same."

Instead of continuing to reminisce, Vivian was silent for a long time, her gaze on the dozens of beach houses passing by outside the window. Just beyond them, the ocean curled gently in and out, small whitecaps announcing each wave.

If Colton didn't know better, he'd say Vivian looked almost melancholy. Impossible. Vivian was always the party girl, the one ready to run off on a wild tear and bring everyone else with her.

"Do you ever…"

Colton glanced over. "Ever what?"

Vivian straightened, back to her usual sassy self, as if the thoughtful moment had been an aberration. "Nothing."

What had she been about to say? And what's more, what was with this mood of hers? Ever since Vivian had arrived in town, she hadn't seemed the same.

Then again, what did Colton really know about what was ordinary for Vivian Reilly? She'd been gone for years, and in that time, she'd surely changed. Just as he had.

They weren't the same old gang anymore, no matter how much they wanted to think they were. The six had grown up, some had gotten married. They were diverging along their own paths now, the kind of grown-up paths that meant it was time to stop reliving a past that couldn't become the present.

Because there were responsibilities waiting in the morning.

A minute later, they pulled up to O'Reilly's, a busy bar in Stone Harbor, the next town over. The distance wasn't much, but it was enough for Colton to feel like he'd stepped away from work. Put some distance between himself and the spotlight of being mayor. Most of the St. John's Cove locals stuck to the town's bars, and few ventured to the neighboring establishments. Here, he felt normal, like a regular guy, not a St. John. It was a nice change, from time to time, just to *be.*

"Tonight when you came by, you seemed like you had something on your mind," Vivian said. "Want to talk about it?"

He could have asked her the same thing. Probed into what was warring within her. There was something…but what it was, Colton couldn't even begin to guess. Once again, he was reminded of how things had changed in half a decade.

Instead he said, "Charlie and Amanda."

Vivian sighed. She'd been around the newly married couple enough in the last few weeks to see what Colton had seen. Heck, astronauts in space could have seen the discontent in the Weston marriage. "Things haven't gotten any better between them?"

Colton shook his head. "Charlie came to me and said they're even talking about divorce. I guess married life hasn't been what they expected."

"Maybe they expected the wrong thing," Vivian said.

Colton considered those words. "Maybe."

He expected Vivian to say more, but she didn't. Instead she seemed again to shift gears, go back to the smiling, teasing person she used to be. She cocked a hip his way and winked at him. "It's kind of quiet in here right now. Maybe we should go out the door and come back in. Really make an entrance."

"That's your specialty." He chuckled. "Remember graduation?"

"Hey, I just wanted to make it memorable."

"My father nearly had you arrested."

"He just didn't get the joke." Vivian laughed, thinking of the horrified look on Edward St. John's prim and proper Bostonian face when she'd roared into the ceremony on a motorcycle, wearing a bikini, a Hawaiian lei and her dark blue graduation cap.

And nothing else.

"Where did you get that Harley anyway?"

"I borrowed it from Jack."

A chill invaded the space between them. Colton backed up. An imperceptible distance, but one nonetheless. "Oh, yeah. I remember now."

It had also been the motorcycle that had carried her out of town, but that time with Jack at the handlebars. Away from St. John's Cove, from her friends, and from everything that she could never have.

Colton crossed to the bar, and Vivian followed. He ordered two light beers, then handed her one of them. "Where'd you two end up?"

"Los Angeles. Jack opened an auto repair shop. He does pretty well." In the semidarkness of the bar, it seemed easy to open up, to share the details of her life with Colton, as if no time at all had passed between them. She wanted to tell him more, to lean on his shoulders, just like she used to.

No. Leaning led to more…and Vivian was *not* going down the path of more.

"And you?"

"I…" What should she tell him? The truth? No. That would only lead to complications, and with Colton, she couldn't have complications. Those would only tie her more to this town, and she couldn't do that. Not to him, not to her. "I work in the food industry."

He chuckled. "Now that I'd like to see. Maybe sometime I'll come out to L.A. and dine wherever you're working."

"That would be nice," she said. Except she wasn't working at a restaurant, not anymore, and the one she did own wasn't on that side of the country. But she kept that to herself. If the day ever came when Colton said he was coming for a visit, she'd find a way to put him off.

She had this night—these last few days before she left to return to L.A.—and that was it.

It would be enough.

"You and Jack…you have a house? A dog?" The words seemed to leave Colton with a painful wince, and for the first time, Vivian wondered if maybe she wasn't the only one with leftover feelings from that summer.

"I'm…I'm not with him anymore," she said softly.

"Since when?"

"Since I caught him with his receptionist. At a bar. Kissing her."

"Oh." Colton's gaze met hers. "Sorry."

Vivian shrugged. "I'm not."

"So are you…?" He let the question hang in the ai

What was Colton asking? If she was single Available?

Oh, this was opening up a can of trouble sh couldn't open, not again. She'd made her decisio five years ago, and she needed to stick to it. For bo their sakes.

Across the room, four members of that night band took their places behind their equipment on th makeshift stage tucked in the corner of the bar. Th drummer raised his sticks, counted off two beat and then the band launched into a toe-tapping rousing rock single. "Want to dance?"

"Are you avoiding the question?"

"Of course not." She shimmied a little to th music. "I'm just in the mood to dance."

"Then we will." He stepped closer to her, and pu out his hand. She slipped hers into his larger palm sending a rush of electricity through her veins. An just like that, before they even made it to the danc floor, dancing together became more than just ex changing a few steps.

Their gazes locked, and even in the darkene room, Vivian knew the look she read in those blu depths. Desire.

They weren't dancing—they were playing wit temptation. Which was exactly what Vivian wa trying to avoid. Colton was on his way—and it was a path that Vivian wouldn't follow. She had to remember that.

Except every time he touched her, or looked at her, she forgot.

The square of parquet flooring crowded with couples, moving in and out, dancing a busy pace to the steady beat of the music. The crush of bodies pushed Colton and Vivian together, his arm settling around her waist as if it had always been there.

"Well?" he asked. "Are you dating anyone now? I don't see a ring on your finger—" he held up her hand as proof "—so I know you aren't married."

"No, I'm not."

"Then…"

The question hung there, and Vivian knew it was more than just a friendly query. They both knew it. "Don't, Colton." She turned away, trying to avoid the question, not just between them, but in his eyes.

"You know, every once in a while, I think back to those days in college, and I wonder why didn't we stay together? I think we would have been good." His voice seemed as dark and intimate as the room around them.

Vivian let out a little laugh. "Come on, Colton. We'd never have worked out."

"Maybe we would. Maybe we wouldn't." He closed the gap even more, and Vivian's pulse began to race. On the dance floor, their body parts brushed, each step making them exchange a feather of a touch. Another. A third. "I can tell you one thing, Vivian."

"What's that?" The words were a breath, and she knew she was definitely in trouble now. Dancing with Colton had been a bad idea. This wasn't fun…

It was *danger.*

"I'd never leave you for my receptionist. And I'd never kiss another woman in a bar."

She swallowed. Damn.

Colton St. John. Too good for her—because he was the good boy, the boy next door, who had aspirations that didn't include her.

She should walk away. Put some distance between them. But she stayed put. "Colton, we'd never…"

"We wouldn't, would we?" He moved a little closer still. In that moment, Vivian realized two things—

Colton St. John was about to kiss her.

And she wasn't going to stop him.

CHAPTER FIVE

KISSING Vivian was like coming home. Like falling into the place where he was always meant to be. His hands reached up, tangling in her auburn locks. Heat rose in the shared space between them and Colton leaned closer, moving to deepen their kiss, to taste even more of the woman he had so long been denied. She was sweet and hot, and everything he'd dreamed of in those years after she left.

She broke away first, each of them breathing a little harder than they had been a moment before. "That's…not dancing."

"No, it's not."

What was that? A bad idea, for sure.

But one he wanted to repeat. Instead he started dancing with her again, trying to make some sense out of a nonsensical decision.

Vivian had made it clear she didn't want a relationship. That she had no intentions of staying in town. He should be glad for that. If he was smart, he'd be concentrating on launching his campaign to run for governor, not on launching a relationship with the one woman he knew who defined complicated emotions.

Not to mention, he knew the dangers of trying to combine a relationship with a political career. He couldn't have it all, and he shouldn't even try. It wasn't fair to him—and especially wasn't fair to Vivian.

Then why did his pulse kick up when he danced with her? Why did he become hyperaware of the undertones of her perfume, the curve of her body against his, the brush of her long hair against his shoulder?

A smile curved up her face. "Close quarters, huh?"

"Just a little." He clasped her free hand in his then brought his cheek to her ear. The scent of jasmine teased at his senses. She was wearing a short, form-fitting black dress. Viv had always been partial to black, curve-flattering outfits and this one was no exception. Colton liked it. Very much. "Too close?"

She shifted against him, and everything that had been simmering suddenly went into a full boil. Colton tightened his hold on her waist, wanting only one thing, thinking not of their friendship, nor of how they were wrong for each other, but only of having her next to him.

And most of all, of kissing her again. And again

and again, until he couldn't remember where their friendship ended and something more had started.

Vivian inhaled, and her chest brushed up against Colton's. She turned, bringing her cheek to his, almost kissing him—almost. "Not too close at all."

He hadn't been the only one who'd enjoyed that kiss, that much was clear. The problem was—what they were going to do about it.

Temptation coiled tighter in his gut. The room dropped away, and all he could hear was the music, the pound-pound-pounding of the music, echoing the insistent beat of desire in his head. His hand ranged up and down her back, and his breath whispered against her neck.

"We should…" she said, then stopped.

"Yeah," Colton said, but didn't move.

"Because we're just…" Another breath in, then out, the warm air raising his awareness.

"Friends," he finished. Friends didn't kiss each other. Friends didn't date. Friends never crossed that imaginary line.

Except the lines had blurred a moment ago, and Colton couldn't seem to get them straight again.

The music pounded, the people around them danced. The world went on, but neither he nor Vivian noticed. "Just frien—"

He silenced her words with his mouth. Vivian curved into him, her body hot against his.

"Hey, Viv! Long time no see!"

Vivian broke away from Colton, and turned toward the voice. Lana Milton, who had graduated with them from St. John's Cove High, stood to the side, with a few other high school friends. "Hi, Lana."

Colton tamped down his annoyance at being interrupted and muttered a hello to Lana. She returned the greeting. "Hey, Colton. Can't believe you became mayor. You're doing a great job, though."

"Thanks."

"My mother says you're the best mayor the town's ever had. And if you knew my mother, you'd know that's saying a lot." Lana laughed, then refocused her attention on Vivian. "I didn't even realize you were in town! It's been so long since I've seen you! We should get together." Lana reached forward, gave Vivian a light jab in the arm. "Hit a few of the old haunts, stir up some trouble."

"Yeah. We should."

"Can always count on you for trouble, huh, Viv?"

A smile skittered across Vivian's face. "Of course."

"How long are you hanging around St. John's Cove?" Lana asked.

"Just a couple more days. I came in for Amanda and Charlie's wedding, then ended up staying for Samantha and Ethan's. But now I really need to get back to L.A." She let out a little laugh. "I never was much for staying in this little place."

So she definitely wasn't staying in town.

Why was Colton surprised? Vivian had nothing tying her to St. John's Cove.

Still after she'd stayed all these weeks, he'd hoped…

Hoped, what? That they could pick up where they'd left off? Maybe rewrite a history that had never had a chance to get past the introductory pages?

"We should do something tonight then." Lana grabbed Vivian's arm, and a wide, devilish grin spread across her face. "What do you say, Viv? Ready to set St. John's Cove on fire? Gotta live up to your reputation, right?"

A second passed, one where Colton was sure Vivian—the Vivian he had always known—would say yes. She'd opt for the good time, running off from this party to that. He started to step back, to let her go, when Vivian shook her head. "Maybe another time, Lana."

Confusion raced across Lana's features. "Uh, okay. Catch you later then?"

"Sure."

"And be sure to give me a call next time you come into town."

"I will." Vivian gave Lana a quick hug, then the two said goodbye.

Once the other woman was gone, Colton turned to Vivian. "You don't have to stay with me. You're only in St. John's Cove for a few more days—you might as well see whoever you can while you're here."

"I'm fine." But she sounded distracted, not li[ke] herself at all.

He put a palm against her forehead. "You mu[st] be sick."

"Me? Not at all."

"For Vivian Reilly to pass up a good time, either t[he] world has turned upside down or you're deathly ill[.]"

"Maybe I just grew up. All of us do, you know[.]" She ran a hand through her hair. "I could ha[ve] become all traditional on you in the last few year[s,] you never know."

"You?" he scoffed. "Never."

"Miracles do happen, Colton St. John."

"Then what was that about over at Hardisty's po[nd] last night?"

"That…that was about trying to see you witho[ut] a shirt on." A tease lit up her eyes, and the shadow[s] that had momentarily filled her gaze disappeare[d.] "Too bad my plan didn't work out."

"Was that all?" Hope rose in his chest, [a] stubborn bobber at the end of the hook she['d] always had on his heart.

He was kidding himself if he thought it had ev[er] really gone away. The last few days had prove[d] that. Hell, that kiss had proven it.

"Of course."

Disappointment curdled in his gut. Why had [he] expected different? Expected things to change? S[he] hadn't been in love with him then—

She wasn't going to instantly fall in love with him now.

Still, Colton had a sense that Vivian had changed, which kept that little bobber of hope from disappearing altogether.

The crowd had merged to the center of the floor, caught up in the frenzy of the beat of a fast-paced song. Vivian and Colton slid to the side, and found themselves tucked in a corner of O'Reilly's.

"What's up, Vivian? You're different," Colton said. "At first, I thought it was just that you'd changed a little, you know, gotten older. But there's more."

She raised one shoulder, dropped it again, the move seeming casual, yet Colton read a note of tension. "I've just gotten older, like you said. But like Lana said, I'm still the same Vivian. Exactly the same."

Except her words lacked the edge they used to have. "No, Viv. There's more to it than that. What's happened in the years since you left? What's happened…" He paused. "To us?"

"We better get back to our table before someone tries to steal it." She spun away from him.

Colton grabbed her arm and hauled her back. She collided lightly with his chest, bringing her mouth within inches of his. Desire roared again within him, and he wondered why he had ever let Vivian out of his life.

What if he had argued with her? Refused to let her go?

He'd never had just friendly feelings for her, and pretending otherwise anymore was a waste of time. "Why did you really leave town?"

She opened her mouth, closed it, clearly surprised by the question. "I hated St. John's Cove. You know that."

He shook his head, then traced along her jaw, watching her eyes widen, her pulse tick in her throat. "You *ran* away. Left an actual dust cloud in your wake. There's a difference."

"I—"

"You ran away from your family. Your friends. From…" He reached up and caught a tendril of her hair, and decided too many years had passed without asking the question he should have asked back then. And finally, the one word came out. *"Me."*

The word escaped with a hard edge, no more being cavalier about the topic, as if the event had been a blip in the radar.

There. He'd said it. For five years, he'd wondered about Vivian, about where she'd gone—but more, why she'd left. The whole thing had been too sudden, the way she turned from acting like she loved him to suddenly cold and distant.

Just like that, one September morning, she'd turned to him and told him it was over. She'd found someone else. She'd never been in love with him. It had all been a summer fling, a crazy temporary crush on a friend.

Friend.

The dreaded six-letter word that Colton had never thought he'd hear again to describe their relationship.

Two days later, Vivian had left town on the back of Jack Hunter's motorcycle, leaving devastation in her wake.

It wasn't just about losing a woman he'd cared deeply about, a woman who had been one of his best friends. It was about the hole in his life, the unfinished chapter in the book. They'd started something, and before it could be finished—

Vivian was gone.

With another man.

And damned if that pain didn't still twinge.

"Why did you do it, Vivian? And don't give me the answer you think I want to hear." He met her gaze. "This time, I want the truth."

"I had plans, Colton, you knew that. I was going to make it big in California and Jack was going that way. So…" She shrugged again, as if this was all no big deal, water under the bridge.

Let it go, forget it. It's over.

We're over.

That's what she'd said back then. *We're over, let it go.* Just like ripping off a bandage, she'd ended the relationship they'd had—if he could have even called what was happening between them a relationship.

Just like five years ago, Vivian wanted Colton to let the subject drop. Except he couldn't, not this time. Because the questions had been raised, and they refused to die without an answer.

The real answer, because he suspected he wasn't getting that. What was she hiding? Why?

"We had plans, too, Vivian," Colton said softly. "Don't you remember?"

Had she seen the way his heart had broken that day? Did she know? Or did she not care?

"I'm not here to resurrect old ghosts, Colton. Just let it go." Then she broke away from him, disappearing into the sea of people. Leaving him behind—just as she had five years before.

CHAPTER SIX

VIVIAN leaned against the brick facade of O'Reilly's, and took in a deep breath. The warm night breeze whispered over her skin, as if trying to soothe her frazzled nerves. It was no use.

Why did you really leave town?

The question still lingered in Vivian's mind, as if Colton were standing beside her, whispering the words again and again.

If only he knew the truth.

Yeah, well, if he did, it would upset the apple cart of his life. Change the trajectory of his future. And she—of all people—wasn't about to do that. Because first and foremost, Vivian Reilly was Colton St. John's friend, and friends didn't ruin other friends' careers, not over something as crazy as a momentary infatuation.

She wrapped her arms around herself, even though she wasn't cold, and started walking down the sidewalk. Was that what had really been between her and Colton? An infatuation?

Or something more?

She closed her eyes, and in an instant, was bac
in his arms on that dance floor, his lips on hers, ho
tempting and oh, so, so good. A heady rush of desi
erupted inside her every time Colton touched he
which told her nothing between them had died. Fa
from it. The years apart had only seemed to inter
sify her reaction to him.

What was she doing here? What game was sh
playing? She couldn't fool herself into thinking ev
erything was over between them. Not after that kis

That meant Vivian had only one choice from
here on out—

To make sure she and Colton returned to th
status quo. Friends only.

"Vivian!"

She turned. As if her mind had conjured him u
out of sheer want, Colton stood behind her on th
sidewalk. "I'm…tired, Colton. I'm going to catch
cab and call it an early night."

*Before I'm tempted to head back inside and pic
up where we left off.*

"Are you ditching me?"

Yes.

"No." She slapped a smile on her face. "Just hav
a lot to do before I head back to L.A."

He caught her hand with his, and the resolve sh
had worked so hard to build began to slip. "Don't

"Don't what?"

"Don't go back. Stay here. What's the West Coast got to offer that St. John's Cove doesn't?"

"My job, for one." Except that was sort of a lie. Her job was technically here. Or could be, if she wanted it to. She could very easily stay and run her ice cream parlor, watch those teenagers' lives transform, see her customers' faces when they enjoyed a double scoop of chocolate mint, instead of hearing all of it secondhand from Kelly. "My apartment, for another." Not that her apartment was much to speak of. She'd been meaning to decorate it for months, years, really, and never quite found the time. The rooms still had that empty, impersonal feeling.

"Both of those are available here."

"My friends."

"You have five good ones right here."

True friends. Five of the best she'd ever met lived right here in St. John's Cove, and every time she saw them, it was as if no more than an hour had passed since they'd last been together. And then there was— "Colton…"

"Stay, Vivian. And finally do what you should have done five years ago."

"What?"

He reached up and cupped her jaw. In the dark, his blue eyes had the depth of a stormy ocean. Oh, how she wanted to just fall into his gaze and never look back.

"Stop running for a minute," he said, his voice as dark as the night, "and give us a chance."

It was the only thing she couldn't do. Vivian left Colton, before the tears brimming in her eyes slipped down her cheeks, and made a liar out of her.

CHAPTER SEVEN

"HI, MOMMA."

The ocean breeze skipped across the grass in the early morning, making the green blades seem as if they were waving. The pain in Vivian's chest eased a bit, and she dropped to the stone bench, bracing her palms on either side of the cool granite.

Three feet away, her mother's name curved across the headstone in simple letters. HELEN REILLY, BELOVED WIFE AND MOTHER. It should have said more. Like taken too soon—while an eleven-year-old Vivian still needed a mother's touch, a firm hand, someone to keep her on track.

And oh, how she still needed her mother's touch. And advice.

Except there wasn't any coming from the cold, hard granite. There was only silence.

Lord knew her father had tried back then, but Daniel had been too caught up in his own grief to pay much attention. Vivian, left to her own devices, had found the best medicine for forgetting—

Trouble.

"I'm sorry, Momma," Vivian whispered, then leaned forward and traced the letters. Even now, all these years later, the rough edges of the stone chafed at her skin, the same as the loss of the woman she had loved so much still chafed at her heart.

The images flashed through her head, fast as slides on a carousel. Her mother, tall and vibrant, her red hair always piled in a messy bun. Laughing—so much laughter. Hel, that's what they'd called her, because she'd been "hell on wheels," the life of the party.

Living with her had been the same. Daniel and Vivian had come home to picnics in the living room, pink paint on the kitchen walls and impromptu twirls around the dining room table. Then, when she was gone, it was as if Vivian had lost her rudder, her way of judging how much fun was too much.

Vivian sighed. "I always meant to make you proud of me."

For too many years, she hadn't done that, had she? She'd chosen the wayward path, instead of the straight and narrow one. But now, perhaps, she would change all that.

"You'd love the ice cream shop. It's just like that one you used to take me to when I was little. Do you remember?" Only silence greeted her, but she knew somewhere, her mother was listening. And, Vivian prayed, smiling. "I might be a little late, but I'm finally getting the hang of being the person you always wanted me to be." She let out a breath. "And, yeah, the person I always wanted to be, too."

From up above, a bird chattered a song. Butterflies flitted among the flowers lining the cemetery's pathways, their multicolored wings bursting in and out of the pink and white petals.

The headstone blurred in Vivian's vision. She brushed away the tears in her eyes. She'd waited too long to come here. Too long to say what she needed to say, whether her mother could really hear her or not.

Oh, how Vivian hoped she could.

The ache for her mother's presence in her life had dulled just a little with the passage of time, but never really disappeared. Every day, she thought of her, and missed her soft voice, her warm arms, but most of all, her calming presence. The way she could walk into a room and smile—and Vivian instantly felt loved. Safe.

Vivian's fingers danced across the granite front, her heart breaking for all those missed years. If she'd known then how much she'd need a mother as she grew up—

But who knows that kind of thing? Who appreciates the ones they love at the time they have them?

"I'm sorry," she whispered again, but the only answer came from the chattering birds.

Vivian leaned back, and settled onto the hard cold seat again. She looked up at the trees, stately oaks, sturdy maples, thick pines, that lined the cemetery with lush greenery. Just over the hill, there was a view of the harbor—the perfect, tranquil setting for her mother, who had always loved the outdoors, and used to tend a small but amazing garden when she'd been alive.

"I should have been that person five years ago," Vivian went on. "Should have told Edward St. John to butt out of my life." She let out a long sigh. "But I had to do the right thing, Mom. Had to do what was right for Colton. I still have to. It's the only choice. He'll be happier in the long run." She paused. "Won't he?"

But would Vivian?

That was the question Vivian had never dared to ask herself. She'd simply said goodbye to Colton then latched on to the first ride out of St. John's Cove that she could find. Never looked back, never considered what might have been.

Because the possibilities were far too painful.

Why did she really leave St. John's Cove?

For Colton St. John. Because she couldn't have him, and she couldn't spend one more day in his arms, living a lie.

A tear slipped down her cheek. "I did the right thing," she whispered. "But oh, I wish there'd been another choice. I wish…"

She reached out to the headstone. "I wish you'd been here to tell me what to do. To tell me it would all be okay."

Because it hadn't been, no matter how much she'd tried to convince herself otherwise. It had been hard and painful, and taken her years to forget the look in Colton's eyes that day.

Now, here she was, back in St. John's Cove, and faced with the same dilemma all over again. Open up her heart to Colton St. John—

Or close it off forever, so he could pursue the political career he'd always wanted.

Deep down, she knew the right answer. The only one that would make Colton happy and ensure his future.

She'd return to L.A., and Colton—

Colton would forget her, just as he had before. He'd move on, move up and along the political ladder. For her, the distance would make forgetting easier. She hoped.

"There is no real choice to make, is there?" Vivian sighed. "There never was. Not then…and not now."

Colton stopped in his office first thing Monday morning, intending only to grab the papers he needed. He paused by his desk, and as he flipped through the stack of papers and file folders in his IN box to get to the ones he needed, a single sheet of paper caught his eye.

He tugged it out, then sat down to read. There wasn't much to see—a few lines of text really—but what he saw surprised him.

And confused everything.

Colton glanced out the window of his office, his gaze traveling along the boardwalk of St. John's Cove, past the bronze statue of his great-grandfather and the myriad of businesses lining the street.

Then he read the paper again—and began to wonder if everything he thought he knew about the people in his life—

Was dead wrong.

Nothing brightened a difficult morning like a bowl of rocky road ice cream. Vivian sat at one of the outside café-style tables at the Frozen Scoop on Monday morning and soaked up the July sun, her face upturned to greet the warm rays.

Why was she still here? She could have caught a flight back to L.A. this morning—and probably should have. After all, she had nothing holding her in St. John's Cove. The weddings were over, the ice cream shop was up and running. She'd spent time with her friends, with her father. She'd visited her mother's grave.

All the untied laces in her life had been tidied up, and as for Colton, well, she knew what to do there.

Then why hadn't she done it? Why hadn't she left already?

If she was smart, she'd get on the first plane for the West Coast, and do exactly what Colton had accused her of doing.

Run away.

Before she was forced to answer his questions. When he'd challenged her, she should have told him exactly the same thing as she had five years ago.

I don't love you. I just want to be friends.

Was she afraid she couldn't get the lie past her throat a second time? Or that she couldn't stick to her resolve with the moon glinting off his dark hair, and the ocean whispering its teasing scent?

"Hey, Viv. Didn't expect to still see you in town."

She turned and opened her eyes, and smiled. "Charlie. Bryce. What a surprise."

Bryce chuckled. A lobsterman, Bryce had the same dark brown hair as his sister, Samantha. "In a town the size of a postage stamp, you're bound to run into someone you know every five seconds."

She laughed. "True." She glanced behind Charlie. "Where's Amanda?"

"Shopping. For the baby. For our house." He shrugged. "I'm not sure what for, really, but shopping. She told me this morning and I already forgot what she said."

"In one ear and out the other, huh? You're a typical husband already, Charlie." Bryce gave him a good-natured jab in the arm.

"Yeah." But the melancholy on Charlie's face

told Vivian that the broken fences between himself and his new bride had not been repaired. She hated seeing any of her friends upset like this, and especially Charlie and Amanda, who had seemed so blissfully happy just a few weeks ago.

A shop door opened and Amanda emerged, her arms filled with bags. Charlie rushed over to take the purchases from her, then the two of them returned to Vivian's table. They didn't talk to each other, and the tension was readable from a mile away. Amanda gave Vivian a quick hug hello, then dropped into a chair. "Phew. I had no idea shopping could be so exhausting."

"Or painful to Charlie's wallet," Bryce said, giving his friends a grin, as he, too, sat down. Charlie ducked inside to get Amanda and himself some ice cream.

Amanda glanced around the table. "We've almost got all six of us together. Too bad Samantha's on her honeymoon. And Colton, where is he?"

The others shrugged. Vivian was glad Colton wasn't here. After last night, she wasn't sure she wanted to see him again at all before she left for L.A.

She should never have kissed him. She'd upset the perfect balance of their friendship, and opened a door she'd slammed shut all those years ago.

But had it really been closed? Or open just enough to leave her heart vulnerable to him again?

"This place is great," Charlie said, interrupting

Vivian's thoughts. He placed two bowls of ice cream on the table: a cherry cordial before Amanda and a vanilla for himself. He took a bite, then smiled. "Best ice cream on the East Coast."

"It's about time we had a place like this in St. John's Cove," Amanda added. "It's perfect for the town. Quaint, but cozy. And cute."

Charlie glanced around at the building and nodded his approval. "It's like whoever owns it really studied the town inside and out. The whole building just fits right in."

"Who does own it?" Bryce asked.

Vivian didn't say a word. Her hand stilled, ice cream halfway to her mouth. Should she tell them? They were her friends, after all. Who else better to understand her need to own this place? To create a place that would recreate the memories of her childhood, and maybe give some to new generations of children?

What was the worst that could happen? People would think the wild child Vivian Reilly was actually a sentimental fool with a weakness for rocky road at heart? In high school, no one had believed Vivian when she'd talked about this dream. But they were older now—surely if anyone would understand, her friends would.

She thought of Colton's reaction when she'd said she'd grown up, become more traditional. He hadn't believed her. He, like Lana, still saw her as the same person.

But what, as he had said, had she done to change that image? Try to entice him to break into the neighbor's pool? Not exactly a way to scream grown-up.

Charlie scoffed. "If Colton's father was still alive, I'd say him. Hell, the man used to own half the town."

Bryce shook his head. "Nah, I really don't see stuffy Edward having a hand in something like this. Besides, this place just opened. And I can't imagine Colton having time to do anything more than his job."

"I agree," Charlie added. "Plus, do you know what Kelly told me? The kids who work here are all at-risk teenagers."

"At risk?" Amanda asked. She'd polished off her cherry cordial and pushed her bowl to the center of the table. "Like, kids who get in trouble?"

"Yeah. Ones who've had a few scrapes with the police. Nothing major, just the kind of kids who need a little help getting turned around and finding their footing." Charlie swallowed a hunk of vanilla.

"I think that's great. Wish there'd been a boss like that around when we'd been in high school." Bryce grinned. "Maybe we would have all stayed out of trouble a lot more often."

The others chuckled. A swell of pride rose in Vivian. Her friends liked the idea, and understood the thinking behind not just the shop, but the teenagers she'd hired to staff it.

Maybe it was time to let people see this other

side of herself. To give up the pretense of being the party girl.

Vivian pushed her bowl to the side. "Hey, guys, what would you say if I told you I opened this place?"

Charlie and Bryce both laughed. "You?" Charlie said. "Come on, Viv. There's no way you'd ever…" His voice trailed off as he took in her face, then glanced back at the shop, then at her again. "You really did?"

She nodded. A flutter of nerves rose in her stomach as she waited for their response. Would it be the same as in high school? Or would they understand? Would they see the new Vivian? The woman she had become in her years away from this town?

"Oh, Viv, I think that's so great," Amanda said. She laid a hand over Vivian's. "Really great. This place suits you. It really does. It's so…fun."

"And what you're doing with those teenagers," Charlie said, a beam of admiration on his face, "just fabulous."

Relief and joy exploded inside of Vivian. She should have said something sooner. Kelly was right. People would understand.

"So you're staying in town? Putting down roots?" Bryce said. "Well, damn, I never thought I'd see the day."

"No, I'm not staying. I bought it, but Kelly Hurley's going to run it. I'm going back to L.A."

"Well, where's the fun in that?" Bryce asked.

"Half the benefit of owning an ice cream parlor is being able to eat all the ice cream you want."

Charlie chuckled. "And going back for extra scoops."

Bryce got to his feet. "Well, gang, I'd love to stay, but I have to get going. I took the day off today for a doctor's appointment. That's no easy feat, if you know what it's like to work with my brothers. I was hoping to sneak in a few quick rounds of golf before I got poked and prodded." Bryce grinned, then put a hand on Charlie's shoulder. "Charlie, you want to go hit the links for a little while?"

Charlie nodded, then leaned over and placed a kiss on Amanda's cheek. The tension between the two still hung in the air, but Vivian read pain in both husband and wife's eyes, as if they wanted to scale the wall keeping them apart, and didn't know how. "I'll be home after lunch."

A moment later, the two men were gone, leaving Amanda and Vivian alone. Amanda's gaze, however, lingered on the spot where Charlie had sat earlier.

"Do you want some more ice cream?" Vivian asked. "I'll pop inside and get you a refill, or make you up a sundae, if you want."

Amanda jerked to attention. "Huh? Oh, sorry. No, I'm fine."

"Charlie's heartbroken, Amanda. You can see it in his face."

Amanda looked away, her heart-shaped face filled

with clouds. "I know. Everyone expects us to be all happy, to be lovey-dovey every second, to go everywhere together, but…" She sighed. "All we do is argue. We're not acting like newlyweds at all. It's like…we can't talk anymore. We try and try, and just go in circles."

"Do you think you got married too fast?"

Tears filled Amanda's eyes, and Vivian wished she hadn't asked the question. "No. I just think maybe we married the wrong people. I mean…I love Charlie, I love him more than anything, but we can't seem to make this work. When we were dating, it was all so easy. We had our own lives, then we had us together, know what I mean? But then we got married, and everything changed. I guess we just got off on the wrong foot, especially with a baby already on the way and everything." She pressed a hand to her stomach.

While they'd been growing up, and in the weeks she'd been here, Vivian had never seen two people more suited for each other than Charlie and Amanda, despite the difficulties they'd been having lately. If those two couldn't make a marriage work—then what hope did everyone else have? She was sure they could fix whatever problems they were having, if they just found the right path. "Have you told him how much you want your marriage to work out? Told him how much all this is bothering you?"

"He knows I want us to work. And he knows

what's on my mind." Then the clouds lifted a little and a light dawned in her eyes. "Well, maybe I haven't said all that in so many words. I mean, I thought he knew me. We've been together so long, and he should just be able to read my mind."

The pink, yellow and white Frozen Scoop sign hung just a few feet away, bright and happy, and the complete opposite of the image of Vivian Reilly. No one who knew her in this town would ever think she had always had such traditional dreams. "Look at this place, Amanda, and tell me how many people who knew me when I was a teenager would have ever guessed that I would open a shop like this?"

A smile crossed Amanda's lips. "Almost none. And I don't mean that in a mean way, just that…"

"I was never the traditional type," Vivian finished, gesturing at her fitted V-neck black T-shirt decorated with a rhinestone beach scene, and dark wash frayed denim shorts.

The clothes she'd brought with her to St. John's Cove because they were what people expected to see on her, not because they were what she usually wore in L.A. Because Vivian had somewhere, deep inside, been still living up to some mental image when she came back home.

"You're right, Viv. No one ever saw you as traditional." Amanda laughed a little. "At all."

"I want this shop, and a few more, if everything goes well."

"A corporate mogul in the making?" Amanda grinned. "Viv, you do surprise me."

"My whole plan was to come into town, open the Frozen Scoop, then leave without telling anyone I owned it. I didn't think anyone would believe that I could own a shop like this successfully."

"Based on your past history."

Vivian nodded. "But what if…" She paused, bit her lip, searching for the right words. For the first time in her life, Vivian Reilly felt unsure. She was launching something new here, something much bigger than a banana split. "What if who I was back then isn't who I really am? What if this—" she waved a hand toward the Frozen Scoop sign "—is?"

"Traditional, but with a touch of fun."

"Exactly." She grinned. Amanda, one of her closest friends, had seen Vivian in the shop. "And no one knows that about me, or that I wanted any of those things out of my life, because I've never told them."

Amanda cocked her head and studied her friend. "Why not?"

Vivian let out a long breath. "That's a long story. For another day. All I want to say is that sometimes people can't tell who you really are, or what you really want, unless you hang up a sign and advertise the real you."

Amanda thought about that for a moment. "You think that's all I have to do? Sit down and talk to

Charlie, and tell him what I really want for our marriage?"

"I'm no expert on long-term relationships, but it seems to me that you've been trying too hard to live up to an image, Amanda, instead of just creating the marriage that works for you and Charlie."

As Vivian said the words, she caught her reflection in the plate-glass windows. The long, wild hair. The dark, tight-fitting clothes. She presented one image, when she really wanted people to see another one. Had she been part of the problem all along? Was she sending out one message and then wondering why people read another?

And then, another person stepped into the picture—

Colton, standing across the street, in front of the Town Hall, dressed in a neatly pressed golf shirt and khaki pants. The visual polar opposite to her. Yet, from across the street, his gaze met hers in the window, and for a moment, she thought she saw exactly the same longing in his blue eyes as she saw in her own.

Maybe Amanda wasn't the only one trying too hard to live up to an image.

CHAPTER EIGHT

WITH half his mind still on his earlier discovery, Colton stood on the steps of the Town Hall, talking with several St. John's Cove residents about the new library. Everyone was excited about the bigger building, the technology that would be available to residents and the expanded book collection to be housed there next spring.

Just as the last person walked away, he noticed someone he knew crossing the street toward him. His pulse kicked up several notches as Vivian neared him. The sun lit her hair from above, making the red tresses seem like they were on fire. His fingers curled at his sides, aching to touch those silky tendrils, to take her in his arms and find out exactly where they stood. Because he was sure as hell tired of being on the dividing line between friends and something more.

"Good morning," she said.

"Hello." A grin spread across his face. "You're up early. I thought you hated early mornings."

"I used to. Now…" She drew in a deep breath, as if soaking up the sunshine and fresh air. "I love the mornings. Getting up, reading the paper, starting my day before anyone else."

Yet another surprise about her. She looked the same, and was trying damned hard to act as if she was the same woman, but Colton got the feeling that a lot of things about Vivian Reilly had changed in the last five years.

She had more layers, more depth, than he'd ever known. Before, he'd dated her, with an eye on a future no deeper than the next few months. He hadn't been invested in his own future back then, never mind his future with another person.

Now, he wondered if Vivian, the only woman who had ever really known him, the only one who had challenged him and dared him to step outside of his comfort zone, could be the one to fill that emptiness in his life.

He'd watched his father, and grandfather before him, ruin their marriages by pouring themselves into their political lives. Their wives had become accessories, not partners. But with Vivian, a strong, decisive woman who had her own life and career goals—

Would his future be different? Could he find the happy medium that had eluded all the other St. John men?

Amanda Weston crossed the street, too, her arms

loaded with purchases. "Hey, Colton. We were just talking about you."

Colton shot Vivian a grin. "You were?"

"Wondering where you were. That's all."

The two women exchanged a glance, and he got the feeling they'd talked about more than his whereabouts. Had Vivian mentioned what had happened last night? How she'd left his questions unanswered?

"Did you happen to discuss anything about any…unfinished business?" he asked.

Vivian's answer came quick, decisive as a butcher knife. "No."

Amanda looked between Colton and Vivian, and the confusion in her eyes gave way to amusement. "Unfinished business, huh? At the rate we're going, the entire Group of Six will be married before the end of summer."

Vivian put up her hands. "Don't look at me. I'm not getting married. I'm going—"

"Back to L.A.," Colton finished for her. "You've said so a hundred times. And yet, you're still here. In fact, you've stayed over a month. That's a long time for someone who keeps talking about heading back. Is that maybe because there's something in St. John's Cove you can't bear to leave?"

Amanda grinned. "I think that's my cue to go. I've got to get home anyway. I want to prepare lunch for Charlie. Something…nice for him to come home to." She put a hand on Vivian's shoulder. "Don't forget to hang up the right sign outside, Viv." Then she left, a smile on her face, and a hopeful, happy look filling her green eyes.

"Wow. Looks like things are improving on the Charlie and Amanda front. What'd you say to her?" Colton asked.

"Nothing much. I told her to stop trying to live up to the image of a happy marriage and just find the one that works for her and Charlie."

Colton chewed that over for a moment, then nodded. "Makes perfect sense. And that's coming from the man who has spent his life measured one way or another by other people's image of what a St. John should be."

"I know the feeling," Vivian said softly.

The shadows had drifted over Vivian's features again, and for the hundredth time, Colton wondered what was troubling her. He gestured toward a picnic table on the boardwalk, and she nodded. They crossed to it and took a seat on either side. The ocean breeze whispered over them, providing a nice respite from the July heat.

Colton put the pile of papers in his hand on the table and leaned forward. "What did she mean about hanging up the right sign?"

"It's…complicated."

He chuckled. "That sounds like you."

"It does?"

"You are a complicated woman, Vivian Reilly. More complicated than people think."

"You're right about that." She let out a little laugh. "And about that sign thing…there's something I need to tell you. That's why I came over to see you." Vivian chewed on her lower lip. He had never seen her this hesitant, and as much as he wanted to reach out and comfort her, he held back, knowing she would say what she wanted—when she wanted. Vivian Reilly was not a woman who could be pushed or prodded.

"You asked me a question last night," she began.

He nodded.

"And I didn't answer you. Then…or now."

"No, you didn't." He leaned forward. "I think I deserve an answer, don't you?"

She nodded. "I…I didn't leave St. John's Cove entirely by choice," she said quietly, the words coming slowly, reluctantly.

Surprise socked him in the gut. "Not by choice? What does that mean?"

"I was…encouraged to leave."

His mind rocketed back to that day, when Vivian had told him that her heart lay elsewhere, to the backdrop of a revving engine and a scowling mechanic at the wheel of the Harley.

Now he wondered…was there more to the story?

"Encouraged? By whom?"

"It's not really about who told me to go, it's about

why. I…" A breeze whispered across the table, ruffling the papers before him, and lifting the top page from the bottom. Vivian glanced down, and whatever words she'd been about to say died on her lips. "What's that?"

He slid the papers to the right, as if moving them would make what was written on them go away. "I was on my way to file my nomination papers for the governor's race."

"Governor St. John." A slight smile crossed her lips, then disappeared. "You're running for governor?"

"I'm a St. John. I've already conquered Mayor Mountain. What else is there to do?" He grinned.

"But…why? I mean, you're already mayor. Why go further?"

"I know, and I've enjoyed that time, but I want…more. I want to make a bigger difference."

"You…you enjoy politics?"

He chuckled. "My father would love to hear me say this, but, yes, I do. I never thought I would. This has been the most frustrating, yet rewarding job I've ever held. I can touch people's lives, and help this town grow."

She cocked her head and studied him. "Are you thinking of going all the way to the top?"

"You mean to president? Like my father dreamed for me?" Colton looked past her, at a place far off, one he couldn't see yet, a horizon still out of reach. "I don't know. I'd like to try. I'm starting with governor, moving on to the senate after that. And then…who knows? All I can say is I love this life. I love knowing my decisions matter. It's rewarding, Vivian. It really is. You see a change in the town, in the people you govern."

A soft smile stole across her lips. "I understand wanting to make a change."

"Then you can see why this career is so important to me."

Vivian nodded and bit her lip, and he swore he saw a tremor of emotion run through her eyes before the shadow flickered away. "You'd make a perfect governor, Colton, just as you made a great mayor. You have all the right qualities. You always did." She rose, her tone as cool and dispassionate as if they had just met, belying the decades of history between them. "I won't keep you then. I have some packing to do anyway." Then she crossed the street and disappeared inside the Frozen Scoop.

Never saying what she'd come to say.

Colton knew then that he'd missed a valuable clue explaining what had happened five years ago. What it was, he still didn't know.

But he wasn't letting Vivian Reilly leave town until he had his answer. Then, they could finally close this chapter of their lives once and for all…or write a new ending. He was hoping for the latter, but pretty damned sure she had her heart set on the first option.

* * *

"Did you tell him the truth?" Kelly asked.

Vivian put her dirty dishes into the dishwasher, then washed and dried her hands. "What good would that do?"

"The man has a right to know, Viv. Besides, it's been five years. Things could be different now."

Vivian knew better. She may have thought, for the last few days, that she and Colton could have a chance at a relationship. Then she'd seen those papers on the table this morning, and it had reminded her all over again why she had left town.

He was going to run for governor. Then senate, on to the presidency. The plan was no different than before, when Edward St. John had sat up late into the night, talking to his son about the political future that could be his. If anything, the stakes were higher today than they had been five years ago.

He was happy. Rewarded by his career. She would never dare to ask him to change paths. Instead she'd do the right thing—and get out of his way.

"If I thought it would change anything, I would." Vivian tossed the dish towel onto the stainless steel counter and let out a sigh. "But if there's anything these last few days have shown me, it's that nothing has changed. And nothing will. Colton is still a St. John—"

"And a St. John shouldn't get wrapped up with a woman who isn't cut out to be Mrs. Mayor."

"Or Mrs. Governor, or First Lady." Vivian ran a

hand through her hair and let out a sigh. She would never be suited for the life of a political wife. Once, she had met Colton's mother—a quiet woman who spent her days serving tea and keeping a perfect house. She had no life, no opinions, and most of all, no spirit left in her. She seemed all…gray and completely unhappy. It was as if being married to Edward St. John had drained the best of Anna's self.

Vivian could never become that woman. She would shrivel up and die if she had to live like that. And how happy would Colton be, married to her if she was like that? No, she wouldn't do that to him. "The best choice is to go back to the way things were."

"Run back to L.A., you mean."

"I'm not running. I'm simply being smart."

Kelly took a long, skinny glass dish down from the shelf and scooped in some chocolate, then some vanilla ice cream. She brought the dish over to the toppings station and slathered on strawberry syrup on one end, pineapple in the middle, hot fudge on the far end, then topped the whole concoction with a generous dollop of fresh whipped cream and a sprinkling of chopped nuts. She slid the bowl across the counter to Vivian. "Here."

"Thanks, but I just had some."

"It's not a snack, it's a life lesson."

Vivian laughed. "In a sundae?"

"Of course." She gestured toward the dessert ingredients. "Here's a group of ingredients you'd never think would go together. Strawberry, pineapple and chocolate? Yet, it works. They find a way to meld."

"I take it this is supposed to be Colton and me?"

"If the dish fits your life situation…" Kelly grinned. "Seriously, Viv, you know the old adage. Opposites attract."

"They can attract, but that doesn't mean they're good for each other." With one fast, hard movement, she pushed the sundae away. The fragile tower of whipped cream and nuts slid down the side and over the edge, puddling on the counter.

Ever since she'd returned to St. John's Cove, she'd had this tiny window of hope, one she'd refused to acknowledge, even to herself until just now.

Hope that maybe this time, she and Colton could find a way, like the sundae melting in the glass dish, to meld their two different personalities, and two vastly different life paths, and finally be together. But as the ice cream melted into a milky mess, she finally faced the truth—

She and Colton were better off apart than together.

Colton had half the pieces of the puzzle, but he knew he was missing the most important one. Vivian had said she hadn't left St. John's Cove by choice.

Someone had encouraged her to go.

Colton couldn't exactly see the motorcycle riding mechanic Jack Hunter telling Vivian what to do. Or her father kicking her out—theirs had always been a close relationship, despite her wild ways. That meant it had to be someone else, someone more forceful. Someone with a reason to want Vivian Reilly out of town.

By four o'clock, Colton had a full conspiracy going. He'd enlisted the Group of Six—all but Samantha, who was still on her honeymoon—as well as Daniel, Vivian's father, to pull off a plan that he hoped like hell would work.

Because he was running out of ideas. And options.

If he didn't move fast, Vivian would return to L.A., and be out of his life again. He could follow her, of course, but he had a feeling that his best chance was here, in St. John's Cove.

Where everything had started.

And everything had ended, five years ago.

At the time, he thought he'd known why. Thought Vivian had left because she'd been in love with Jack. But now, he wasn't so sure. Ever since she'd been back in town, nagging doubts had plagued Colton, telling him far more had been behind Vivian's sudden departure. Now he knew for sure.

He glanced around the massive house he had lived in ever since his father's death, the same Victorian that had housed three generations of St. Johns. The emptiness echoed.

Colton decided he had had enough of that. If he

could find a way to make things work with Vivian, maybe…

Maybe this house would find the kind of happiness it had never really enjoyed before.

"I'll have her there," Amanda promised on the other end of the phone, drawing Colton out of his thoughts. "Seven-thirty, right?"

"Yep. And remember, tell her it's a get-together for the old gang. I want this to be a total surprise. Really sweep her off her feet."

Amanda laughed softly. "Who knew you were such a romantic at heart, Colton St. John?" Then she hung up, leaving Colton to finish setting up his diabolical plan to win Vivian Reilly's heart.

CHAPTER NINE

THE scent of baked clams, lobster, corn and potatoes carried on the air like a scent beacon, drawing Vivian down the old wooden steps and onto the beach. As soon as she hit the sand, she slipped off her flip-flops. Her bare feet sank into the soft white granules, the feel of the beach as familiar as the back of her hand. Her skirt swung around her ankles, chased from side to side by a gentle breeze.

Waves whooshed in and out, nature's soft music. A few feet down the beach, Vivian saw the flickering orange flames from the campfire, and she picked up her pace. A real New England clambake—a treat, something she hadn't been able to enjoy in years, considering New England clambakes weren't exactly plentiful in California.

Her stomach rumbled in anticipation as she made her way down the beach. "Hey, gang, this should be a great last get-togeth…"

The words died in her throat as she took in the

romantic tableau waiting for her. A thick plaid blanket, anchored by white candles in jars. Daisy petals scattered all over, like confetti.

Daisies. Her favorite flower. Only one person knew that detail.

In the middle of it all, not the other members of the Group of Six, as she'd expected when Amanda had called her a little while ago and invited her to a beach party, but just one person—

Colton.

Vivian paused a few feet away. If she knew what was best, she would turn around now. Let him go, just as she had five years before.

But this time, the letting go wasn't happening as easily. Maybe because she knew how painful it was going to be. How much she would miss him. Her resolve faltered, along with her steps.

"Don't go," Colton said, as if reading her mind.

"Colton—"

He stepped forward, and took her hand. "I've got clams, and lobster. Made them myself." He grinned. "You have to at least stay and appreciate the fact that I cooked for you."

She laughed. "I do appreciate that."

"I bet you're wondering where everyone else is," Colton said as he led her toward the blanket.

Vivian took a seat on the soft plaid fabric. *Don't stay,* the little voice in the back of her mind warned her. *Leave now, before you get in any deeper.*

She didn't move.

"Are they coming later?" Even as she asked the question, she already knew the answer. And still she didn't move.

"Nope. Tonight is just about me. And you." Colton reached into a silver bucket, pulled out a chilled bottle of white wine, then poured two glasses, handing one to Vivian. "Amanda, Charlie and Bryce were all part of my plan to get you here. Oh, and your dad, too."

She shook her head. Her father. Of course. She should have known. "Under that gruff exterior, my father is a bigger romantic than you. Don't let him fool you."

Colton chuckled. Then he paused, his gaze roaming over her. "You look beautiful. I like you in white. It's very different."

She smoothed a hand over the lace top and the cotton skirt. "This…this is what I normally wear."

He arched a brow. "It is?"

"Back in California, yes. I'm not the same there as I was here." She rose and turned away. Her feet sank into the soft sand. "I just wanted you to see that side of me before…"

"Before what?"

She had to say it. Had to cut this off now, before she got in any deeper than she already was. But the scent of the clambake called to her, inviting her to come back, to put her plan on hold. Forget for one more night.

She couldn't. Colton was like a dessert she knew she shouldn't have…yet she craved nonetheless. "Before I say goodbye," she said. "We're better off friends, Colton."

There. Start to break the news to him. He'd heard it before. Maybe this time he'd believe her—

And she'd believe herself, too.

"Now, see, you keep on saying that, Vivian, but I don't buy it. Not anymore." He put down his wineglass, then leaned forward and cupped her jaw. Everything within Vivian began to hum with desire. "And you know why?"

She shook her head, mute.

Where were those words she needed so desperately to say? The speech she had prepared in her head this afternoon? Gone…lost somewhere in the sea of wanting Colton.

"Because friends—" he leaned in closer, so close she could see the reflection of the stars in his eyes "—don't kiss friends the way you kiss me."

She wanted to protest. She knew she should protest. But she didn't.

Instead she did a very Vivian thing—stirred up more trouble. By kissing Colton St. John back.

Colton had thought the first time he kissed Vivian after five years apart had been amazing. He'd been wrong.

That kiss paled in comparison to this one. Every

touch of her lips rocketed desire through his veins, quadrupling the impact on his senses.

She curved against him, her body fitting into his with the ease of someone who knew him well. His hands slid along her silky skin, then tangled in her hair, that wild mane of hair that teased at his senses every time he saw her. The scent of jasmine whispered along her skin, tempting him.

Vivian let out a soft moan, and ranged her hands up his back, sliding them beneath his shirt. When her warm palms met his skin, Colton groaned. Damn. It had been so long, too long—

Their kiss deepened, tongues dancing, Vivian drawing even closer as if she couldn't get enough of him. Colton's hand slid up between them, then beneath the fabric of her T-shirt to cup her breast. The soft mound fit perfectly in his palm, just like every part of Vivian.

"Vivian, I want you," he whispered, then kissed her lightly, "not just now—" another kiss "—but tomorrow—" another kiss "—and the next day—" a kiss trailed down her neck "—and the one after that…" now along the pulse ticking in her throat "…and every single one beyond that."

Vivian broke away, and slid back. "Colton, we should stop. Before—"

"Before what? Before we fall in love?"

"We won't do that, Colton."

"Why? Because we already have and you don't

want to admit it? Or because you still want to keep telling me we didn't fall in love that summer, either?" He leaned closer, searching for the truth in the flickering firelight dancing in her eyes. "Or did we? And you just lied to me about how you felt?"

She recoiled, as if he'd slapped her, and he wanted to take the words back, but they needed to be said. All these years, he hadn't confronted her about the way she'd ended their relationship, as if she had an on-off switch on her heart.

Then she recovered and let out a laugh, but the sound shook. "You know me, Colton. I'm not one for settling down."

She hadn't quite answered the question, he noticed. But he let it drop for now, and pressed forward with another. "Or for doing crazy things like opening ice cream shops?"

Surprise widened her gaze. "How did you know about that?"

"I'm the mayor, Vivian. I know about everything that happens in this town. I see every business license that gets filed in town, so I can keep my finger on the pulse of St. John's Cove." Colton withdrew from Vivian, and turned instead to the tarp covering the clambake. He began removing the rocks and seaweed that had kept the seafood and vegetables insulated while they cooked. "So, why didn't you tell me about opening the Frozen Scoop?"

And what else haven't you told me?

Because he knew she was hiding something. What, he couldn't tell. And why, he didn't know. The Vivian he had always known had held no secrets, had been as open as a book, especially with him. But in the last five years…

She'd become a different woman, and damned if he could understand why.

She shrugged, then looked away. "It's no big deal. Just a little ice cream shop."

Colton tipped Vivian's chin and waited until she met his gaze. "It's not just a little ice cream shop, Viv. It's the dream you've had ever since you were a little girl because your mother used to take you to that little shop in Hyannis every Sunday, just her and you. A special treat."

Tears pooled in Vivian's eyes. "You remembered."

"I've been friends with you forever, Vivian. I remember everything."

"Colton…why do you have to do that?" She pivoted away, and hurried down to the beach, her back to him.

Colton followed her, but stopped when he saw the glisten of tears on Vivian's cheeks. *Vivian* was crying? Vivian, the strong one, the tough girl, who never betrayed a moment of vulnerability—

Crying?

Why? What had he said? Done?

He reached for her, drawing her into his arms, but she remained stiff, unyielding. His mind ran over everything she'd said in the last few weeks, trying to assemble the pieces into some kind of reasonable sense. "Is this still about the ice cream shop?"

"No."

"Because I think it's a great idea, I really do. And I know when we were in high school I said something really stupid when you read that essay about it. I don't remember what I said, but trust me, I was a teenage boy. Smart and out-of-my-mouth didn't go together back then."

"It's not that. Really." She heaved a long sigh, one that seemed to have the weight of the world in it.

The tide began to work its way in, dark water lapping at their toes. Soon, the water would extend its reach up the beach, and what had once been exposed would disappear for a few hours. Colton had the feeling if he didn't get to what was standing between him and Vivian right now, it would be like the beach—back under water and unreachable.

"I know you lied to me that day, the day you left. And I know someone made you leave, but you don't want to tell me who or why. Am I right?"

She nodded. Finally confirming what he had always known, deep in his gut. The truth whispered in the back of his mind, but he needed Vivian to confirm his suspicions.

Gently Colton turned Vivian until she was facing him. "Just tell me one thing."

"What?"

"Were you in love with me back then?"

Vivian hesitated, and in the quiet of that moment, dread twisted Colton's gut into knots. "Yes," she whispered. "Yes, I was. Very much."

His heart sang. She *had* loved him after all. Somewhere in that answer, there was hope that they could work all this out. "Then why, Vivian? Why did you leave?"

She turned away again. "Colton, don't ask me that. Please."

"I am asking, Vivian. And I'm not leaving until you answer me."

She shook her head. "You have plans for your future, Colton. Plans that don't include me." A sad smile slid across Vivian's face, then disappeared. "I'm not cut out to be a politician's wife, Colton. You should know that. I wasn't then, and I'm not now. If we'd stayed together then, can you imagine what that would have done to your political career?"

"What do you mean?"

"Me, Colton, of all people? Come on, be realistic. The girl who shows up in a bikini at graduation? The girl who helped you put the principal's car on the roof of the high school? Are you going to use that in your campaign speech?"

"Of course not. I don't know why you're worried about that, it's all past history. We live in the present, and today, you're not running around in a bikini. You're running an ice cream shop."

She shook her head. "You know as well as I do that the public's memory is long and detailed. And what about the media? They love to dig up that kind of thing. Your campaign will be ruined before you put up your first yard sign. So why don't we just be realistic now, rather than drag this out and make the ending more painful?"

He let out a laugh. "Is that what this is all about? You don't want to be the mayor's wife? Don't want to be married to the governor? Hell, I'll step down today. Withdraw my election papers. Then we can hop on a plane to Vegas in the morning. Get married, live happily ever after."

She put a hand on his arm and met his gaze. "Do you really want to do that? You've worked your whole life toward a political career. You told me yourself you love this job, that it fulfills you. This is who you are, Colton. Don't throw it away for me."

"Vivian, I love you. I don't want this without you."

He was doing exactly what his father had predicted, and if she didn't stop it now, Colton would walk away from his job and his future. Five years down the road, or ten, would he still be as happy, knowing he'd thrown it all away, for her? Or would he blame her for the choices he'd made?

"I've got a life back in L.A.," Vivian said. "I don't want to live in St. John's Cove. And yes, Colton, I was in love with you once, but I was young then and…" She let out a breath, and with it, the shards of her heart as it broke with the telling of yet another lie, "I'm different now. We both are." She leaned forward and pressed a quick kiss to his cheek, tears searing at the back of her eyes. "I'll see you the next time I'm back in town. Good luck with the governor's race."

Vivian packed the last shirt into her bag, then zipped the suitcase shut.

"You're getting real good at this," her father said. He'd taken a position in the doorway about five minutes ago and had yet to leave.

"At packing? It's not rocket science, Dad."

"No. At leaving." He crossed into the bedroom— the same bedroom Vivian had had all her life—and took a seat on the green-and-white comforter and watched Vivian set her bags by the door. "Don't you think it's about time you did some staying instead?"

"Dad—"

"Don't 'Dad' me. You know I'm right. You've got nothing waiting for you back in California except an empty apartment. Here, you have family, friends, a business." He paused. "Colton."

"*Dad.*"

"Didn't I just say not to 'Dad' me?" Daniel shot her a grin, then propped his elbows on his knees and leaned forward. "You get one shot at life, honey. Don't waste it aiming in the wrong direction."

"I'm not."

"You are if your heart is here and you're flying there."

She sighed and dropped into a white wicker chair. When she'd been ten, she'd sat in this chair every night before she went to bed, scribbling silly dreams in her diary. Then her mother had died a year later, and she'd stopped scribbling anything. That was the day she'd realized she had to be realistic, about her life, about her future. She was doing the same thing right now. Even if realism hurt like heck. "I can't be the kind of woman he needs."

Daniel waved a hand in dismissal. "How do you know what kind of woman Colton needs?"

"You've met his mother, Dad. She's the perfect politician's wife. And me…" Vivian let out a laugh. "I'm *so* not."

"Says who?"

"Edward St. John, for one."

"What does he have to do with anything? He's been dead three years."

"He told me how awful I'd be for Colton's political career."

Daniel's face tightened. "That man had the gall to say something to you?"

"It's why I left, Dad." Vivian let out a long breath. She'd held all this inside for so long. She was tired of keeping the secrets to herself. What good had they done, really, except drive her to the other side of the country? Despite what she'd said to Colton, she'd realized in the last few weeks that she did miss St. John's Cove. Her friends, her family, heck, even the Clam Digger restaurant. She might not be able to have Colton, but maybe she could spend more time here, with the other people she loved. She knew, though, that she could only do that if she stopped hiding from the real reasons she left. "Back then, Colton and I were so much in love. I know Colton was thinking marriage, because he mentioned it a couple of times. I guess his father must have found out, because Edward came to the diner where I was working one afternoon and told me I'd never be the kind of woman his son needed."

Her father muttered several unflattering things under his breath.

Now that the story was out, she might as well tell it all. "And…he offered me ten thousand dollars if I'd leave town."

This time, her father didn't bother to keep the unflattering words under his breath. "If he was still alive, I'd kill him."

"I didn't take the money. I didn't want his money. I didn't want anything from him."

Her father rose and paced the room, his face red. "How could he do that? Say that to you?"

"He was watching out for Colton's interests." She drew in a breath, let it out and faced the truth. "For years, I've been blaming Edward for my leaving. But honestly, he was right."

"Right? The man was a jerk, saying things like that to my daughter."

"Maybe, but he had a point. I was always in trouble back then. I didn't have a clue about living conventionally. All I wanted to do was—"

"Escape." Her father let out the word on a long, heavy breath.

Their gazes met, shared pain unfurling between them. "Yeah."

Vivian picked at an invisible piece of lint on her jeans, then smoothed the denim. "I wasn't cut out back then to be the wife of the mayor. The wife of the governor? Or God forbid, the First Lady? Leaving Colton was the best thing I could have done for his career."

"And what about for you?"

She lifted her head to meet her father's gaze, tears burning in her eyes. "I survived."

He harrumphed. Then he sat down on the bed, across from her. "What would be so wrong about you as the governor's wife? Or even better, First Lady? I think you'd be great."

"You're my father, you're supposed to say that."

"No, I'm supposed to tell you the truth. And you, my dear—" he reached out and brushed a lock of hair out of her eyes, making her feel ten again "—would be a breath of fresh air. I'd rather have you than some cardboard yes-wife at the side of the politician I vote for, any day."

She laughed. "Lord knows I'd never be a yes-wife."

"And you've changed, Vivian. Look what you're doing with those kids who work for you. Amazing stuff. I wish someone like you had been around when I'd been raising you. Those are the days when I missed your mother. Still do." His voice caught on the last few syllables.

"Dad, you didn't do such a bad job."

"I could have done better. Could have been there."

Vivian's eyes misted, and she reached for her father's hand. Age had put lines in the back of the strong hands that had done everything from build her a bookcase to change the tires on her battered first car. The same hands that had bandaged her knees and taken her picture at graduation. He'd been a great father. More than she could have asked for. "You were, Dad. And you're here now."

His smile wobbled, and he swiped at his face. "Got something in my damned eye," he said, his voice as gruff as sandpaper.

"Yeah, me, too."

After a minute, Daniel cleared his throat. "Vivian, I don't care what that fool Edward St. John said to you back then. You're made of the kind of tough stuff we all need more of. I'm damned proud of you, and…" His gaze met hers, and she saw the tears had never really gone away. "I know your mother would be, too."

"She'd be proud of you, too," Vivian whispered.

Then she reached forward and drew her father into a hug. One that lasted until every one of Vivian's doubts had been erased.

It took Colton five minutes after he'd watched Vivian walk away from him yet again to put the pieces together. He called Amanda and Charlie and offered them a romantic clambake on the beach, complete with all the fixings, if they wanted it. "Sure, we'd love that," Charlie said. "But I thought you made that for you and Vivian."

"Things didn't work out as I planned."

"Sorry, man. Anything I can do?"

"No. This is one problem I have to take care of myself. Enjoy the lobster."

"We will." As Charlie said goodbye, Colton heard a lightness in his friend's voice that he hadn't heard in weeks. Clearly his marriage had improved, and things were on the right track. That made for two happy endings among the Group of Six—Samantha and Ethan, and now Charlie and Amanda.

Colton was holding out for one more.

CHAPTER TEN

VIVIAN looked at the address on the paper Bryce had dropped off at her father's house a few minutes ago, then shook her head. It had to be a mistake.

She got out of the car, her steps slow and cautious. Night had fallen, the only light coming from the moon overhead.

Bryce hadn't said anything more than "Go here," before running back out to his car. The message had been as mysterious as the destination. She started to turn back to her car when she heard someone call her name.

"I hope you brought your swimsuit."

Colton.

Vivian pivoted back. She couldn't see him in the dark, but she would recognize his voice anywhere. "Don't tell me you're in that pool, because I'll never believe it. Did you…climb over the fence? Actually break the law?"

"You'll never know if you don't come in here yourself."

"Where's Ely?" She looked around, but the house was still and dark. "Colton," she said, lowering her voice to a whisper, "you really shouldn't do this. If you get caught, it would be awful for your career."

"Vivian Reilly, are you going to keep asking questions or make me throw you into this pool myself?"

She laughed, then grabbed the tote bag she'd packed for the beach earlier, slid past the open gate and into the fenced-in pool area. "Okay, I'm here."

"Now change. I won't talk to you unless you're in the water, too."

"Colton—"

"Don't tell me you're frozen with fear with a little challenge?"

"Who, me?"

She could almost hear him smirk. "You have fifteen seconds, Vivian Reilly."

Vivian grinned. Maybe the Colton she'd remembered hadn't disappeared after all. "I only need ten."

She ducked into the small shed Ely had beside the pool and changed into her swimsuit, then slid into the water. Silky warmth covered her body, enticing her to dive under.

When she came up for air, Colton was there.

As he'd always been. All her life. Colton St. John, the one man she could depend on, the only man who had ever really had her heart.

Vivian looked around. Still quiet and dark. "Am I going to get shot?"

"Not tonight," Colton said. "This time, I'm older and wiser than when I was a teenager. I called Ely in Florida and asked his permission to use his pool. Even called the neighbors and told them what I was doing so no one would call the cops."

"You did? How did you ever convince Ely to let you use his pool?" She treaded water gently beside Colton, the warm water sluicing over her skin.

"I told him my girlfriend was really hot, and she needed a way to cool off."

She arched a brow.

"Truth? I reminded Ely that the new library is going to have a special Civil War history section, the thing he lobbied hardest for, and he owed me a favor or two." Colton shrugged. "Plus, Ely is head of the historical committee, and he's…kind of become a friend of mine."

"Ely, a friend? I guess the residents of St. John's Cove have changed since I've been gone."

He moved forward and slid a hand up her bare back, teasing at the edge of her bikini top and sending a shiver of desire down her skin. "Not all of them. At least not in the ways that count."

She laughed, then slid into his arms. With a couple of kicks, they were out of the deep end, and into shallower waters. But that didn't stop the building heat between them, quadrupled by the silky feel of the water. "I'm glad to hear that. But…"

"What?"

Vivian sobered. Back at her father's house, packed suitcases waited for her. And here in St. John's Cove, Colton had a political future waiting for him. Regardless of what she might want, she had to do what was right—for him. She'd seen how much this job, this town, mattered to him. "This is all great for one night, but in the morning, you're still the mayor and I'm still the girl who got you into trouble faster than you could count to ten."

"And I still don't care." Colton reached up and cupped her jaw, then kissed her, deeply, thoroughly, telling Vivian with his mouth, his touch, how he felt.

Every second in his arms was as wonderful as the last, and Vivian wanted to believe that this could work. She really did. Vivian drew back. "You really want a woman who rides a motorcycle in a bikini in your life?"

"I definitely want a woman in a bikini in my life. As long as you promise only I get to see you wear it on the motorcycle. Because otherwise I'll have every voter in town following you…right out of town, if you do that again." Then he kissed her again, and a third time. "I love you, Vivian Reilly, in a bikini, in a snowsuit, in whatever you want to wear or do. I've loved you for as long as I can remember. And I always will."

Her heart leaped in her chest. She had waited so long to hear those words, and not just from anyone, but from Colton St. John. He loved her—

And not just as a friend. Even better, he loved her just the way she was.

Still, Vivian hesitated. "Listen, Colton, you should know what happened five years ago."

"My father was the one who told you to leave, wasn't he?"

"How…how did you know?"

"I put the pieces together. First, I asked myself who would do such a thing? Then, who would be the only person who could tell you what to do. It all came back to one answer—my father. The only question I have is why. Why you would ever think I would be better off without you than with you."

"It was the right choice then," she said. "I wasn't ready to do anything except leave and grow up."

He brushed a wet tendril of hair off her cheek. "I guess we both did a lot of growing up during those years, didn't we?"

She nodded. "And we changed."

"We did." His gaze met hers. "Too much?"

Had they changed too much? The question hung between them. She thought of Colton's commitment to his career. His love for politics, not because he wanted to win, but because he wanted to change lives and communities.

But wasn't that what she was doing, too, only on a smaller scale? One cone at a time? "No, not too much."

A grin spread across his face. "I'm glad to hear that."

"One thing *has* changed, though."

The grin faltered. "What?"

Now it was her turn to surprise him—one more time. She smiled up at him. "I'm not afraid to tell you I'm in love with you, too."

He hauled her to him. "Oh, God, Vivian, you have no idea how long I've waited to hear you say that." He kissed her, this time thoroughly, until she could no longer see straight. He released her, the grin planted firmly again on his face.

A small round object bobbed nearby in the water. Something round and inflated, from what Vivian could see. She moved to push it away, when Colton stopped her. "Uh-uh. I wouldn't do that if I were you."

"Why?"

"What's on that floating drink caddy—" his eyes twinkled in the moonlight with a mischievous glint "—is the biggest Dare ever."

"A Dare?"

"Yep. And if you thought the trouble we got into years ago was big, it's nothing compared to what I have planned for you with this."

This was the Colton she remembered—the one she loved—the man who teased and tempted, who had brought as much fun into her life as she had tried to seek. He was still there, and hadn't been lost in his political career.

They were still the same people—only older, wiser, more mature. She could still have the Colton she had always known, the one who, in those difficult years after her mother had died, had been not just a friend, but a salvation. Because he'd made her laugh—and that had made her forget.

That had been the beginning for her, the first days when she'd fallen in love with him. For taking care of her when he didn't even know he was. Later, she'd tell him about that—

After she found out what was in that floating caddy.

She reached out a hand, then pulled it back. "Big trouble, you say?"

"The biggest."

Vivian pretended to think. "What kind?"

Colton reached into the well of the drink caddy, then took Vivian's left hand with his own, holding it up out of the water. "Do you dare…to become my wife?"

She inhaled sharply. The ring—a one-carat round stone—caught the light from the stars and sparkled softly as Colton slid it onto her finger. At first, the jewelry felt foreign, out of place. Then a moment later, absolutely perfect. "Wife?"

Colton grinned. "The biggest trouble ever. The kind that spells a permanent hitch." His hand closed over hers, and he narrowed the gap between them. "You could have your ice cream shop in St. John's Cove, and at the end of the day, come home to your husband and our kids. Just like you wrote about."

"You were listening."

"I told you, Vivian, I remember everything about

you." He kissed her lightly, then trailed several kisses along her jaw. "You're a pretty unforgettable woman."

"What about being governor?"

"*If* I win…how would you like to take what you're doing with those kids at the Frozen Scoop and do it on a state level?"

She hadn't even thought about having influence as a politician's wife. That she, of all people, could have a positive impact. She thought of how the teenagers working for her had changed in the last few weeks, and what a difference she could make if she could multiply that by ten kids, a hundred…a thousand.

This, Vivian realized, was what she had been working toward all these years. It was as if every step of her path had been leading her to this. To Colton. To a life together, changing the world one person, one town at a time. She smiled. "I think I could start learning to serve tea."

Colton laughed. "Just be who you are, Vivian, and that'll be perfect."

Then he took her in his arms, and with one more kiss, cast a vote for the only term of office he wanted in Vivian's life—

Forever.

⊚ ROMANCE 2-in-1

Coming next month

CINDERELLA ON HIS DOORSTEP
by Rebecca Winters

When Dana arrives on location at Chateau Belles Fleurs, she becomes the star of her own real-life fairy tale. Complete with handsome prince, irresistible chateau owner Alex.

ACCIDENTALLY EXPECTING!
by Lucy Gordon

Dante doesn't believe he has a future to live for. So he knows the spark between him and Ferne can be no more than a holiday romance. Until Ferne discovers she's pregnant!

AUSTRALIAN BOSS: DIAMOND RING
by Jennie Adams

Fiona's sunny smile and bouncy enthusiasm are a breath of fresh air in Brent's office and his ordered world. Is Fiona the woman to finally release Brent's fears and the secret he's lived with all his life?

LIGHTS, CAMERA...KISS THE BOSS
by Nikki Logan

Growing up, Ava was like a sister to TV producer Daniel. Now she's a stunning woman and ratings winner. Dan can't take his eye off the ball now and risk losing a promotion, or can he?

On sale 5ᵗʰ February 2010

Available at WHSmith, Tesco, ASDA, Eason and all good bookshops.
For full Mills & Boon range including eBooks visit
www.millsandboon.co.uk

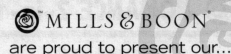

are proud to present our...

Book of the Month

An Officer
and a Millionaire
by Maureen Child
from Mills & Boon®
Desire™ 2-in-1

The broad-shouldered military man had no
patience with games. Margie had to go. She'd
been masquerading as his spouse and living in his
house. Now all his skills were focused on payback:
he'd have that "wedding night"!

Enjoy double the romance in this
great-value 2-in-1!
An Officer and a Millionaire by Maureen Child and
Mr Strictly Business by Day Leclaire

Mills & Boon® Desire™ 2-in-1
Available 18th December 2009

Something to say about our
Book of the Month?
Tell us what you think!
millsandboon.co.uk/community

*The only woman he wanted –
and the one he couldn't have…*

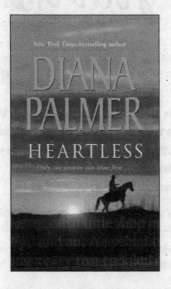

When a moment of unbridled passion results in a
kiss, wealthy ranch owner Jason realises that he's
falling for Gracie. But Gracie harbours a shameful
secret that makes her deeply afraid to love. Stung by
her rejection, Jason leaves, ready to put the past –
and the one woman he can't have – behind him.

But when danger threatens, Jason will have
her heart forever!

Available 5th February 2010

www.millsandboon.co.uk

millsandboon.co.uk Community

Join Us!

The Community is the perfect place to meet and chat to kindred spirits who love books and reading as much as you do, but it's also the place to:

- **Get the inside scoop from authors about their latest books**
- **Learn how to write a romance book with advice from our editors**
- **Help us to continue publishing the best in women's fiction**
- **Share your thoughts on the books we publish**
- **Befriend other users**

Forums: Interact with each other as well as authors, editors and a whole host of other users worldwide.

Blogs: Every registered community member has their own blog to tell the world what they're up to and what's on their mind.

Book Challenge: We're aiming to read 5,000 books and have joined forces with The Reading Agency in our inaugural Book Challenge.

Profile Page: Showcase yourself and keep a record of your recent community activity.

Social Networking: We've added buttons at the end of every post to share via digg, Facebook, Google, Yahoo, technorati and de.licio.us.

www.millsandboon.co.uk

WEB/M&B/RTL

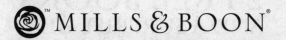

MILLS & BOON®

www.millsandboon.co.uk

◎ All the latest titles

◎ Free online reads

◎ Irresistible special offers

And there's more...

◎ Missed a book? Buy from our huge
   discounted backlist

◎ Sign up to our FREE monthly
   eNewsletter

◎ eBooks available now

◎ More about your favourite authors

◎ Great competitions

Make sure you visit today!

www.millsandboon.co.uk

2 FREE BOOKS
AND A SURPRISE GIFT

We would like to take this opportunity to thank you for reading this Mills & Boon® book by offering you the chance to take TWO more specially selected books from the Romance series absolutely FREE! We're also making this offer to introduce you to the benefits of the Mills & Boon® Book Club™—

- **FREE home delivery**
- **FREE gifts and competitions**
- **FREE monthly Newsletter**
- **Exclusive Mills & Boon Book Club offers**
- **Books available before they're in the shops**

Accepting these FREE books and gift places you under no obligation to buy, you may cancel at any time, even after receiving your free shipment. Simply complete your details below and return the entire page to the address below. You don't even need a stamp!

YES Please send me 2 free Romance books and a surprise gift. I understand that unless you hear from me, I will receive 5 superb new stories every month including two 2-in-1 books priced at £4.99 each and a single book priced at £3.19, postage and packing free. I am under no obligation to purchase any books and may cancel my subscription at any time. The free books and gift will be mine to keep in any case.

Ms/Mrs/Miss/Mr_____ Initials _____

Surname _____

Address _____

_____ Postcode _____

Send this whole page to: Mills & Boon Book Club, Free Book Offer, FREEPOST NAT 10298, Richmond, TW9 1BR

Offer valid in UK only and is not available to current Mills & Boon Book Club subscribers to this series. Overseas and Eire please write for details.. We reserve the right to refuse an application and applicants must be aged 18 years or over. Only one application per household. Terms and prices subject to change without notice. Offer expires 31st March 2010. As a result of this application, you may receive offers from Harlequin Mills & Boon and other carefully selected companies. If you would prefer not to share in this opportunity please write to The Data Manager, PO Box 676, Richmond, TW9 1WU.

Mills & Boon® is a registered trademark owned by Harlequin Mills & Boon Limited.
The Mills & Boon® Book Club™ is being used as a trademark.

Ho

Th
sh
rei
qu
ite

6/9

**Reader favorite Cara Colter
and *New York Times* bestselling author
Shirley Jump bring you**

JUST MARRIED!

*Wedding bells are ringing in St John's Cove
and we're about to see love blossoming
for the bridesmaid and the best man!*

Praise for Cara Colter:

'Cara Colter's HIS MISTLETOE BRIDE
has everything: wonderful characters,
humor and emotional depth.'
—*RT Book Reviews*

Praise for Shirley Jump:

Shirley Jump always succeeds in getting the plot,
he characters, the settings and the emotions right.'
—*Cataromance.com*

C0000 002 474 861